# Breaking Beauty

# Breaking Beauty

*Stories edited by* Lynette Washington

First published 2014 by MidnightSun Publishing Pty Ltd
PO Box 3647, Rundle Mall, SA 5000, Australia.
www.midnightsunpublishing.com



Cataloguing-in-Publication entry is available from the
National Library of Australia.
http://catalogue.nla.gov.au

Cover and internal design by Kim Lock

Printed and bound in Australia by Griffin Press. The papers used by MidnightSun in the manufacture of this book are natural, recyclable products made from wood grown in sustainable plantation forests.

The production of this book was assisted by the
Creative Writing Department
at the University of Adelaide.

*For Mark, Ryan and Kathleen*

# Contents

**Introduction**
Brian Castro . . . . . . . . . . . . . . . . . . . . . . . . . . . . . . . 9

**Dear Reader** . . . . . . . . . . . . . . . . . . . . . . . . . . . . . . 12

**This is the Body of Wonderful Jones**
Amy T. Matthews . . . . . . . . . . . . . . . . . . . . . . . . . . . . . 14

**A Well Strained Fence**
Corrie Hosking . . . . . . . . . . . . . . . . . . . . . . . . . . . . . . 18

**The Window Winder**
Stefan Laszczuk . . . . . . . . . . . . . . . . . . . . . . . . . . . . . 29

**Triangles, Squares and Circles**
Ruby Ewens . . . . . . . . . . . . . . . . . . . . . . . . . . . . . . . 37

**Beautiful Girl**
Gillian Britton . . . . . . . . . . . . . . . . . . . . . . . . . . . . . . 45

**The Beholders**
Sean Williams . . . . . . . . . . . . . . . . . . . . . . . . . . . . . . 55

**O Lucky Man**
Lesley Beasley . . . . . . . . . . . . . . . . . . . . . . . . . . . . . . 59

**A Simple Matter of Aesthetics**
Rebekah Clarkson . . . . . . . . . . . . . . . . . . . . . . . . 63

**Duck**
Bryan Whalen . . . . . . . . . . . . . . . . . . . . . . . . . . . 75

**Ladies Tea Party**
Lilliana Rose. . . . . . . . . . . . . . . . . . . . . . . . . . . . 79

**To My Son**
Matthew Gabriel . . . . . . . . . . . . . . . . . . . . . . . . . 90

**Antiques**
Bernadette Smith . . . . . . . . . . . . . . . . . . . . . . . . 99

**Olive/Oliver**
Jessica Clements . . . . . . . . . . . . . . . . . . . . . . . . 105

**Roses for Lungs**
Annabel Evitts . . . . . . . . . . . . . . . . . . . . . . . . . 110

**Pissing Blood for Lucy Liu**
Rachael Mead . . . . . . . . . . . . . . . . . . . . . . . . . . 117

**Wabi-Sabi**
Katherine Arguile . . . . . . . . . . . . . . . . . . . . . . . 127

**Self Portrait with Angel Olsen**
Bryan Whalen . . . . . . . . . . . . . . . . . . . . . . . . . . 133

**Thank You, Jean Harley**
Heather Taylor Johnson. . . . . . . . . . . . . . . . . . . . 138

**The Blood, the Snow, the Raven**
Katherine Doube . . . . . . . . . . . . . . . . . . . . . . . . 145

**Lia and Amos**
Lynette Washington . . . . . . . . . . . . . . . . . . . . . . 149

**All You Need Is Love**
Anna Solding . . . . . . . . . . . . . . . . . . . . . . . . . . . . . . 153

**A Paper Woman**
Melanie Kinsman. . . . . . . . . . . . . . . . . . . . . . . . . . . . 165

**Something About Religion**
Reg Taylor . . . . . . . . . . . . . . . . . . . . . . . . . . . . . . . . 174

**Whatever Happened to the Fairytale Ending?**
Mary Lynn Mather . . . . . . . . . . . . . . . . . . . . . . . . . 186

**The Abduction of Ganymede**
Gay Lynch . . . . . . . . . . . . . . . . . . . . . . . . . . . . . . . . 189

**A Real Looker**
Jo Lennan. . . . . . . . . . . . . . . . . . . . . . . . . . . . . . . . . 201

**Athina and the Sixty-Nine Calorie Burn**
Rosemary Jackson . . . . . . . . . . . . . . . . . . . . . . . . . 209

**Walking with Alice**
Kimberley Zeneth . . . . . . . . . . . . . . . . . . . . . . . . . 221

**Acknowledgements** . . . . . . . . . . . . . . . . . . . . . . . 227

**Thank You** . . . . . . . . . . . . . . . . . . . . . . . . . . . . . 227

# Introduction

## Brian Castro

I'm writing this introduction before the onset of temporary blindness, burning the candle at both ends as *tempus fugit* and I'm in-sighted by verbal misuse of the very best kind—incited by what good writing does to anyone devoted to it, namely by the short story, which is making a comeback both subtly and in your face, and wondering why it ever went away, perhaps because we were too imbued with the great whatever novel in the Borealis of canons or by the glossy fits of fashionable shades of grey—and I thought of Dorian Gray, lingering there in American spellcheck, cursed by a beauty that could only be literary— and I thought yes, *fugit*, these are very good stories—not exactly a curse to ward off the sceptics and curmudgeons decrying the *global creative writing style* but in simple admiration for the fleeting and the fleeing before one's eyes, as a good short story is wont to do, not allowing its meaning to fully emerge because that would kill it, but letting it flit mothlike into memory; and so a detailed synopsis would not do here, but suffice to say the beauty of a story is embedded in a reader's eyes which act in concert with paint-stripper, revealing what is beneath the wallpaper or the figure within the carpet-bagger, and these stories do *reveal*, by heavens, inflated boobs and that Jones girl next door, the hacked technology of the bionically beautiful, the bountiful effects of over a decade of masterful and doctoral grooming, of the first and best creative writing college in the country—dare I say this as a stable-hand—which has *taken stock,* surmounted the odds; though let's not look at names invidiously but sample the way these works accrue in an interior dialogic between tasters of language and mores, of trespass and licence, for they tell us where the mood is at—as a compass not boxed by Keats, but by Rousseau, when he said that there was nothing beautiful except that which did not exist, not as a thing forever but stories as elastic bands which snap us back to a reality from the thin stretch where violence and love manifest in very different (second) takes, for what is the Real anyway…beauty, beholder and eye coming together in schlock hyperbolic zombification…the way love and death both occur in a moment of inadvertence, when God takes his hand off the tiller, when there are those 'small clandestine frenzies' or when one is playing possum—oh let the mist fall from our eyes about beauty—and so the shapes of lives and of cities and of countries, are triangulated through frissons and maps, divining rights through all kinds of rhythmic conversations of love, which like any other addiction, morphs into tough, traitorous, romantic and remedial: breaking bad, breaking even and breaking beauty; and the *distance,* the measure of separation, of icy clear-sightedness between subject and material is to be lauded in this collection because *here* is the pivot, the tipping-point between polemic, hatred, contempt and the redemption of literature, and whether it be gender-crossing, cross-dressing, class-cruising, you name it, the psychological authenticity is exceptional, executed in economical prose which is supremely and simply *aware,* not only of the here and now but of what went before, *readers* demonstrating how much skill and schooling they have as *writers;* these are crafty wordsmiths indeed, from the top shelves, professionals who give you paramedic knowledge about Faulknerian density, suicides and relationships; daughters dissecting mothers and daughters, sons anatomising fathers and sons, sons and lovers, but mothers…yes, it might not hurt to say that women rule: it's been too long in the coming to readily see another side of consciousness without ho-humming an ideology, to instead satirise or ironise with the same lethal weapons at Flaubert's disposal by deploying both direct and indirect free speech to achieve crystal-hard tones where undercurrents swirl beneath the finality of a phallic finial and the folly of the *nouveau-faux* in the suburbs of hell…and of course I'm *in-speaking*, because what good is an intro-duction if you haven't been in-ducted, or even read the stories—well, I'm refusing to capitalise on that fact, but all reading is retro-accumulation, and writing is the back-slash of a sword, not yet murderous, but the fire next time, my friend; so I'm confident in saying many of these stories make up a deep-water jazz articulating the fissures of the ocean floor, poetically echo-sounding what cannot be expressed in academic-speak; and if we feel the deep need to find missing flights therein, then here they are, the armies of the night, the cohorts of grace, the future asylums of literature and language.

# Dear Reader

## Lynette Washington

The reason this book is in your hand or on your screen right now is because of a series of serendipitous moments. Coincidences and near misses, coagulations of fortune. A friendship built on a mutual love of books and writing became a publishing partnership based on a mutual love of books and writing when Anna Solding invited me on a writing retreat to Meningie in the South Australian Coorong.

In that peaceful and productive environment I said to Anna: *I would like to edit a collection of stories written by University of Adelaide Creative Writing postgrads. You did it—how can I make it happen?* Conversation flowed, as it does on writers' retreats after periods of intense communal—yet separate—creativity; in the spirit of camaraderie and understanding. Anna encouraged me to run with the idea: *If you edit it, I will publish it,* she said. Kim Lock, a talented writer and graphic designer who was on the retreat said: *I'll do the cover!* If there was ever a beautiful moment—of fortune, collegiality, trust and mutual respect—that was it.

It wasn't hard to decide on the theme. Beauty is all around me, every day. When I wake and my daughter has crawled into bed to give me a cuddle—I open my eyes and there is her silky hair on my pillow. When my son gives me his best smile—the one that cracks open my heart so that warmth oozes all through me. When the sun shines in winter, when I hear a song that is just right for *that* moment, when I smell Mum's cooking, when I witness a man being gentle with a sobbing child.

It's true that beauty is everywhere, and often in the small things.

However. Complementary forces are at play, ideas are interconnected and interdependent. Dualities allow us to understand things that are otherwise meaningless. There is no beauty without ugliness. We need to crack beauty open, we need to break it, to really understand it.

Dear Reader, from *that* came this book. Brimming with twenty-eight stories by writers who I admire and adore, whose words have moved me to tears and laughter and who I feel privileged to have worked with. Each of these stories has something to say. Some say it quietly, others do not. Some make you lean in, others make you stretch out. Some will inspire you, others will break your heart. Some will feel familiar, others strikingly alien. Complementary forces indeed, proving that without darkness there is no light.

I hope that you see beauty when you turn these pages, and where there is no obviously shiny surface layer in sight, lean in. You will find it. It is there. It is everywhere.

# This is the Body of Wonderful Jones

Amy T. Matthews

This is the body of Wonderful Jones. She's five feet, five and a half inches. Her legs are long and her waist short. She is thin but not skinny; she does six hours of cardio a week and three dance classes. She is strong. Her chemical tan accents her hipbones and defines her quads and abs. Her breasts are as hard and round as basketballs; when she moves they seem to bounce loosely beneath the skin, as though they're not quite a part of her. She paid $12,000 for them. They're her third set of implants. Her nipples sit on them like cherries on a sundae. Underneath the lower curve of the basketballs are silvery scars. Her hair is a mass of extensions in five shades of blonde; her roots are dark. In the posters and centrefolds and on the covers of the DVDs she wears short skirts with no underwear underneath. Her bum is small and somehow vulnerable looking. Her face is the same orange-gold as her body; with eyebrows plucked into surprised arches, fake eyelashes bristling like hairy spiders, a mouth that's overstuffed and soft with collagen, waxed baby pink, and eyes which are as flat as the plains back home.

This orange woman with her fake hair, fake tan, and fake name is twenty-seven years old. If you divide the number of films she's made by the number of years she's been alive, it comes to 2.5 films per year. In those 68 films, she's kissed 132 girls, gone down on 102 of them, sucked 97 cocks, had 60 of those cocks enter her (17 of them anally), been cuffed and whipped, play-raped, spanked, and fucked in every possible way. At no point do her eyes change. She stares glassily into the camera, her sticky pink puffy lips open and emit low animal noises, which are supposed to suggest pleasure.

She's won best female performer at the industry awards six times, as well as awards for Best All-Girl Sex Scene, Best Anal Sex Scene, Best Group Sex Scene, Best Threeway Sex Scene, Best Solo Sex Scene, and Most Outrageous. She's also famous for being the nude pin up on the wall in the latest Fringedwellers film clip. She was dating the lead singer at the time. When he was finished with her she fucked the bass player in an attempt to make him jealous. He didn't care. The bass player's wife did.

Earlier this year, Wonderful Jones checked herself into Rehab. Not any old rehab. *Celebrity Rehab*, the television show. She spent most of the series walking around in a semi-transparent white singlet. Without a bra. Her website had several million hits; her 68 films set some download record. Wonderful Jones crossed over into the mainstream. And suddenly her body was everywhere. She was on the cover of *Zoo*, staring at me as I paid for my petrol at the gas station; she was in an ad for diet energy drinks: *I'm not sweet but I've got plenty of kick.* She was in a zombie movie, walking around with blood splattered all over her basketball tits.

But worst of all, she was in my bedroom. I'd only been sleeping with Harry for a month, but I'd loved him for the best part of a year. He was five years older than me, beautiful, the coolest guy in the office. I thought we were friends. And when we started fooling around, I thought he was getting serious. He acted like he was serious: we saw each other every night; he sent me playful text messages, he told me he wanted me. And if the sex wasn't the best I'd ever had, it wasn't the worst either. At least until the night he yelled her name. *Wonderful!*

I couldn't get out from under him fast enough.

'What did you say?'

'What?' He looked shifty. His cock was still erect and it twitched, looking like some pathetic blind fleshy worm.

'You called me Wonderful.'

'I said you *were* wonderful.'

And I knew by the greasy light in his eye that he knew. I'd seen that light too many times before not to recognise it. 'I'm not her.'

He ran a hand through his dark hair and gave me an irritated look. 'Would you come back to bed? You're being weird.'

I hated him for his irritation, for the way he lied to me, and most of all for that glistening ugly cock of his. 'Get out.' I threw his clothes at him.

'You know you're mental,' he sighed. But he didn't protest. He covered himself up. And then he did what most of them do. On his way out he couldn't resist slapping back at me, 'You're not as hot as she is.'

After he'd gone I cried. Then I threw up. Because the body of Wonderful Jones is my body; she'd come slithering out of the womb with me: my twin. In every single one of those 68 films, my body, genetically identical in every single way, was licked and sucked and whipped and fucked. Millions of people had seen this body—my body, her body, our body—naked. And every time a man came home with me, I wondered if they were thinking of her. If they wished I had the basketball implants, instead of the natural boobs she had in the first six films. If they wished I was oranger, thinner, fatter-lipped. If, as they fucked me, they were pounding her, the girl who waited for them on their computers late at night; the girl they called up on their iPhone whenever they wanted to have a wank. My sister. Wonderful.

---

**Amy T. Matthews** is a Lecturer in Creative Writing at Flinders University and a Research Fellow in the Discipline of English and Creative Writing at the University of Adelaide. She was the winner of the 2010 Adelaide Festival Unpublished Manuscript Award for her novel *End of the Night Girl*, which was published by Wakefield Press in 2011. *End of the Night Girl* was shortlisted for the 2012 Dobbie Literary Award and the 2012 Colin Roderick Award. Her most recent book, *Navigating the Kingdom of Night*, was published by the University of Adelaide Press in 2013.

# A Well Strained Fence

## Corrie Hosking

Slashing. And then finally along the fence-line. A thing of great beauty, a well-strained fence. There was the sound of the tractor for five hours, forty three minutes (seconds: too transient to document accurately—although when I first looked down at my watch it was eighteen). Discounting the seconds, it was thirteen minutes past lunchtime. I did not have hunger. I would not have stopped for lunch today as I was too busy in my thoughts and I'm no longer so troubled by that happening. But at 12:43 (and eighteen seconds) Jean was mid-row C12 with a sandwich.

She said What's going on? I've been standing here waving for minutes.

I stopped the engine. Some people say 'killed'—I 'killed' the engine. My Mother would have said it is a figure of speech. I found the rubber band in my pocket, but I did not need to pull it over my hand to my wrist.

Jean said Don't get upset now Jim.

I said How many minutes.

She said You know it doesn't matter, so please don't get upset. You're disorientated. It's all right. It's lunchtime. You worked through. It happens. I just need to hurry up and get back to my work.

I said How many minutes.

She said Five.

I said Is that an estimate, as I am aware people exaggerate their approximation of time when they are irritated.

She said All right it was more like two minutes, but that's still a guess and anyway it's not important.

I patted my pocket for the rubber band again. I could feel it was twisted.

She said Are you all right to have lunch?

I said Thank you for the sandwich. Is it ham and pickle? I got out of the tractor.

She said We can eat right here. It's not too hot. Put your hat on. Yes, it's ham and pickle. She looked at me sideways. Are you all right, Jim?

After lunch it was different. The afternoon was slow. I thought about the slasher slicing through each blade of grass in slow motion. There was some panic that I would never get things back in synchronicity, that I would have to spend the rest of the day, week, month, year picturing all that grass being sliced. I finished slashing the Chardonnay block and I stopped the tractor, but I did not 'kill' the engine, I put the tractor in neutral and got my rubber band out and held it, considered pinging myself three times quickly and thought of what Jean would say. She would say It's not important. You can think of something else. Don't get upset, Jim. Sing 'Heads and shoulders, knees and toes' right through, touching your body parts as you sing and move on to think of something beautiful. The time was 3:05. I would not sing a children's song. I set my eyes on my most satisfying fence—posts perfectly upright in relation to the ground, wires exceptionally taut in their strain. I put the tractor into first and got going again. Jean makes it all right, because she knows what's real.

Near knock off I had finished the day's allotted slashing.

The area looked tidy. I like it to look tidy. I nodded at the even grass and re-tucked my shirt. Grand-Pa used to say that a real man lived for his work, lived for the land, loved it. My Mother said Grand-Pa drove my father to drink. The drink was alcohol. A lot of it. A lot of it and a person gets drunk. A lot of it over time and a person gets damaged—in the brain, which can greatly affect function, thoughts, feelings and memory and internally in the organs, most commonly the liver. Mother said the drink killed my father, but Jean says That's bullshit, your dad killed himself. Grand-Pa showed me a pig's liver six weeks before my eighth birthday. It was large and glossy and had a smell that made my lip hook up over my teeth and my feet take me reeling back. Since then I don't like to let myself think of the innards. Jean says there is no need for me to—unless I am physically unwell. Then she says it's good to be informed and men aren't typically very responsible when it comes to their health. It is very complex and messy inside.

A real man lives for his work. I keep Grand-Pa's words in my head. Grand-Pa had model cars and he gave them and the farm to me when he died. I had to wait ten years until the place was legally mine. That is the law. After he read the will, Father said every filthy curse he could muster and then some that did not make sense to me as a boy of age eight. Mother spoke to me behind her hand, her breath hot. There, there, Jimmy-James. There, there… It's not your worry. Father's angry about Grand-Pa's will—about being absent. If he could get ahold of himself, examine his rage, he'd have to admit the anger was more about himself. Mother said Grand-Pa wanted hard work and the farm to flourish, but Father was always obstinate in the face of Grand-Pa's ambitions for him and now it's more than too late... For some there'd be grief with the loss of a loved one. But God only knows what there is for your Father. My Mother was big, floral-clad and a ruddy-faced squinter. She said she was born on the land, for the land and lived by the laws of the land and that meant Having your feet firmly on the ground, your head on your shoulders and not taking any rubbish from nobody. She said the laws of the land weren't always good to the womenfolk and she said she had to be bigger and tougher than Father for all our sakes. My Mother cried when things were hard for me and held me with her arms which were big from years of bread-making. I can remember the woman-smell of being near her armpits when her flesh pushed into my ears to block out Father's ruckus. I cannot be sure how I received Mother's explanations at that time. It is a difficult mental exercise to remember back into my eight year old body with my fine skin and bony elbows. That was a time when Father was the most bad and Jean says probably when my troubles really commenced. There was the belt. And that particular corner of the woodshed. The smell of possum piss and sawdust still make my guts quiver…

Much later, when the official documentation was signed and my name was in bold type on the Title, Mother said another memorable thing. Father's car was not in its place over the oil stain and Mother was under the front veranda slumped against the door, hair damp and springing at her temples. She spoke almost below my hearing and I recall looking about to check if I was really right there next to her and being addressed. With God as my witness, I'm that sorry for the way of these years. Children should grow up barefoot, free and cushioned with love. Not skirting the edge of their father's vision, backs to the wall in fear. What a Hell of a mess… Mother found my eyes and seemed shocked—like she did not know me or I was a person she was not expecting.

There were magpies picking over the cut grass. I had been

stood on the hill for sometime, just looking out over things, thinking it tidy. A crow called. I looked for it in the scrubby patch of Eucalyptus Leucoxylon I had planted nine and a half years back to control erosion. When Jean first moved out here with me she said crows sounded like they were cursing. From that moment it changed how I heard them. Fuuuuck…fuuuck…fuuuuuuuuckkk Jean laughed. I didn't like how that moment changed something for me, but Jean said it was just a funny way of thinking about it. I do not do cursing. I like things still. I do not let a muscle twitch in my face. I learnt how to stop the chaos of my body when I was ten. Mother put rubber bands around my wrists and she would ping them when she saw me quaking. After a while—maybe four to six months, but I am unsure of the exact time as I did not note this as a boy—I learnt to ping the rubber bands myself. I still keep one rubber band in my pocket. Most commonly I only need to think about it. Occasionally I need to use it. Jean described it as this: Maybe it brings you back to your body. I said more-or-less yes (like my Mother used to say). Jean said my Mother was well before her time and very clever. Jean would have liked to meet my Mother before the ageing got her and her brain started to decay and she was forced by the fly-in-fly-out doctors to go into a secure home and spend her days wheeled in front of the television sucking on barley sugars and talking to anyone who'd listen about catching the train into Adelaide. Well before her time, Jim—to have thought up the rubber bands and using that snap to bring you back. I still imagine the feeling of flicking my hands like before I was ten. That feeling is like flinging off spiders or something dirty.

There are a lot of spiders in the vineyard. One day I liked the look of the threads being pulled by the tractor. They were very silver and captivating to observe in the sunshine.

That day was different because Jean did something private and surprising and she said it was all right to do it and that it would help me to relax and she was right because for a couple of hours I was different. She laughed at my pants round my ankles, lily-white legs messy with hair, my socks and boots still on. On the ground in the twist of my clothes I told her I feel like I'm a small boy again, before everything got so violent and complicated and I felt the sun sink deep through my skin to my blood and the smell of the vines was very strong. I was not worried by Jean interrupting my spray schedule. But then later that afternoon the sprayer broke and I had to take a trip to town and the part had to be completely replaced and would have to come from Perth and I stared at my boots and thought hard about my rubber band while Bob was leaning on the counter watching me.

As their webs get disturbed the golden orbs are very quick to head back for the vines. They are good at looking after themselves and starting again. Occasionally there is one on the windscreen and I look at its underbelly and delicately patterned legs. I am glad for a windscreen. A cabin. You can keep clear from any of the messiness and discomfort of nature. After a day in the tractor, the webs collect along the side of the windscreen—so many that they form a thick sticky rope. The first time I saw this I was very taken aback and near-ran back to the house to get Jean. When I am dreaming and driving through the spider webs, I imagine they are gradually entrapping me. I know spider webs cannot stop a tractor. I did not have a good education in mathematics or physics—the teacher had a bad odour, his slacks were too high and his preoccupation was not with the patterns in numbers or the formula for explaining phenomena, but the closeness he could get to the females in the class. Despite the lacking in this education, I understand spider dragline silk to have a tensile strength of roughly 1.3 GPa. There is argument in the general community around spider web being stronger than steel, but it is a common mistake to confuse strength and toughness when comparing to other materials. There are some who have calculated how spider web could stop a particularly fast American train, but these equations are beyond me to apply to my own situation with an 80 horsepower tractor travelling at 6km/hr. I don't know why my brain spirals into this type of thinking, particularly as I often find the thoughts to be uncontrollable and therefore unpleasant.

This type of commotion in my thoughts first started after I became accustomed to driving the tractor, many years back. In the early stages I was attending only to the mechanics—learning the particular hum, whine and grind of engine and gear changes, balancing clutch and throttle, experiencing an unfamiliar engagement of my trunk as I sat upright in the sprung seat, riding the undulations of the vineyard, somewhat like being in saddle, horseback, establishing the best sequence of moments to get efficiently round the end post once I had come to the end of a row. All this and more became unconscious in time. I was glad for this, as I see this as the way of men I have watched. My Grand-Pa could clear a fence, even as an old bloke. A few brisk steps, his left hand on a fence post and his body hurled or swung over. Such a trick, my Nan would say. Such thick wrists, I would note and apparently no overcrowded thoughts to get in the way of approaching such a physical feat. Which foot where…how fast…bumps in the earth…where to bear weight…when to bring up the arm…abrasion of the old Red Gum post…an ant upside down on the wire…

So as I thought less about the driving, my brain began to seek out different activity and at times it was not thoughts of my choice. At first I fought the dreaming because it made my heart race and my lungs not suck enough air. It was a hard fight because the troublesome thoughts kept coming to me. The resistance had me exhausted. I told something about it to Jean and she said it was ridiculous to fight, that: It's precisely what brains do. They think, they dream, they work things out. It's a quite lovely thing, Jim. Let it happen. She said maybe it was my subconscious trying to tell me something. I said I don't want to think about that. She said, Jim, in the way she does with her head tilted and her eyes looking up from under her eyebrows. It's a look that I have learned to recognise. It means she believes me to be fixed in my thoughts. She asked me to tell her more about the spider webs. I said No. It's just silly thoughts, like kids dream up. She said Thoughts are never silly. Thoughts are very powerful and it helps to work out where they come from and what they mean. She said something else about men thinking differently and I said, All I know is although women can wear the pants, they have bosoms and certainly no block and tackle (which is an expression my Grand-Pa used). Jean always laughs when I say block and tackle. Her laugh makes the breath come slowly out my nose and my shoulders relax. Once I asked why she'd want the trouble of me. She said Jim, yes you are complicated and some would even say odd. But you've had a Hell of a life—like a lot of us have, in one way or another. Despite all the shit, you're good and honest and you let me be. She put her hand to my face and said, You're also quite lovely—particularly because you're utterly unaware. Her hand against my face was cool and dry-moist like a grape leaf and the troubles got a bit less tangly in my head.

To stay on track you have to be organised. Things need to be in their place. Tools: mattock, shovel, rake, crow bar.

Picking, pruning, electric snips. Sulphur, copper hydroxide, glyphosate, sprayseed, DMIs. Dripper pieces. Staples. Wire: 2.65mm. Engine, hydraulic, gear oil and so on. I reversed the tractor into the shed for the night. I swept off the tyres (which is unnecessary, but one of my habits). Also you need to organise your thinking to function satisfactorily. Vineyard: 7:30am to 5:00pm. Sub-category: Specify variety, block number, row number. Jean marks individual vines with pink ribbon. My preference is for numbering. The seasons change things. That's called the Big Picture. You can't change the Big Picture, but you have to alter the Little Picture otherwise there will be no control in the vineyard. It has been a long time coming, this vineyard. I had no idea it was what I would end up doing with the farm.

I first saw a vineyard at the pictures. It was just a short film about Grape Growing Around the World—there were often short films about some form of agriculture at the local cinema. I was most interested. I admired the order of the rows, the neatness possible in nature. It was so much more understandable than a paddock of wheat. Each plant could be known and numbered and part of a section or block. Each plant was allowed growth and fruiting and then it was cut back to a knowable state for the Winter. It was a most brilliant moment, seeing that short film. I said to Mother I was very interested. But it was more than that. Maybe it was something like a Strong Emotion. Maybe something like Beauty. I said to Mother, I should like to know that more fully. And she found me a book. I learned all I could about vineyards and many folks laughed and made reference to wine and alcohol—that Mother had best watch out as the thirst was in the blood. Mother came close to me—as she did. She said, Pay no mind to that. They just don't understand. Jimmy-James, she always said, You are just you and that is right and good. Before she lost her mind, she'd like to remind me that I used to sit at the table at dinnertime and recite facts I had learned from that book.

> San Gimignano on the fringe of Chianti makes a good dry Vernaccia. Michelangelo is quoted as saying that it 'kisses, licks, bites, thrusts and stings'.

Good grief! my Mother would laugh.

Concluding I quoted, Such lively tasting notes are rare.

It was never about the drinking or the alcohol or the wine for me, that's why the paragraphs I can still quote are so amusing says Jean.

So at twelve, six years before the farm was officially mine, I had put in five acres of Chardonnay and I had done it by hand and the efforts had required more food and water intake than I had ever experienced and I had moved through having sore hands, to bloodied hands, to scabby hands, to calloused. My mother said I had grown into a fine farming lad. My father did not speak much on the matter, but after Mother organised a contract with a large company in the Barossa and I sold my first ten tonnes, Mother pushed him up to where I was standing on the rise overlooking the vineyard and he said, It's a good job, Jim. A bloody good job. Wine may well be a drink for the new Australians and the bloody silver tails, but you've done a bloody good job applying yerself to the task. And Mother said, Your father is proud of you, Jimmy-James. That's what he's trying to say, isn't it Bill? Very proud. We both are.

I swept the veranda round the shed in the way I do. Big strong strokes to feel the heat behind my shoulder blades. I put the broom in its place and I checked the position of the tractor. It was straight enough. Plenty of access for tomorrow.

There were spider webs across the headlights. I stood for a moment. I felt the worry as Jean has taught me to do. It takes practice every single day. I thought of her. She would be at the kitchen bench after finishing her day's work. She'd have the meat marinating, but not with too much spice and I would do the potatoes. I pulled the sliding door across the shed, hooked the padlock, used more pressure than practical to lock it. I'd use WD40 on the mechanism tomorrow.

---

**Corrie Hosking** started out writing for theatre, enjoying various awards, grants and scholarships. She finished a PhD in Creative Writing at The University of Adelaide and consequently the draft of her first novel, *Ash Rain,* which went on to win a Festival Award for Literature, was published by Wakefield Press in 2004 and saw her named one of The Sydney Morning Herald's Best Young Novelists, 2005. Her second novel, *Eating Lolly* was published by HarperCollins in 2008 and she is still attempting to write her third—a book for children, (which essentially just rips off what's been happening in her own family, raising four small people). She also has a real job as a Paediatric Social Worker and likes to think she is involved with the running of 26 acres in the Adelaide Hills.

# The Window Winder

## Stefan Laszczuk

About ten years ago I used to do some labouring work for a friend of mine. Not real work. Just a couple of days of cash-in-hand odd jobs. I didn't really have much clue as a labourer so he mainly had me running errands. It wasn't a particularly memorable period of employment per se, but there was one job he sent me on that I will never forget. It was the last job I ever did for him. After that job, life was never quite the same.

The last thing I had to do one sticky Friday afternoon was return a ladder he had borrowed from this bloke who owned a recording studio. Truth be known, I don't know why he borrowed that ladder in the first place. It was a piece of shit. Like the music this bloke listened to, it was heavy and metal and old. The steps were actually jagged, sharp even. You couldn't even stand on it unless you were wearing a decent pair of boots. It would literally cut into your feet. It was virtually useless. But if my mate hadn't bothered to borrow it ten years ago then I never would have seen what I saw that day. And I wouldn't understand beauty and tragedy and the way that sometimes they are the very same thing.

My street directory was from 1985. This bloke's recording studio was on a street that didn't exist in 1985. I had to guess where it was from the blank spaces on the outskirts of the directory. My mate had described the building for me. 'Big and wooden,' he'd said. 'Number 35. Lovers Lane.' And he'd given a cheeky wink.

I'd driven all around where I thought Lovers Lane could be and I was about to give up when I came across a street-post without a sign on top. I remember hearing once that Lovers Lane was apparently the most stolen street sign in the English speaking world. I don't know how they worked it out, or if there is a list of the most popular stolen street signs kept somewhere as a matter of public record. All I know is that I remembered that inane fact as soon as I saw that signless post, and so on a hunch I turned left, down that nameless street and scanned around me.

If it was Lovers Lane, I thought to myself, it was a damn insult to the name. There were no parked cars with necking teenagers anywhere. It was all dirty industrial graffitied buildings and poorly designed car parking spaces with overgrown weeds pushing up through gaps in the badly laid concrete slabs. There were bars over the factory windows and a slight bitter smell that leaked in through my partially open window.

And then I noticed a large wooden warehouse-looking building at the far end of the street. Thinking that it must be what I was looking for and thinking, at the same time, as I pressed my foot to the floor, that the bitter smell was starting to become unslight, I reached down to wind my window up. I drove a panel van—it was old enough to be my street directory's father—and the driver's side window winder had always been a bit dicky, even at the best of times. I should have known the day would come when it would fall off.

I suppose I should have slowed down before looking for it somewhere under my legs on the floor. I suppose I might have taken my foot off the accelerator, perhaps even applied the brake—perhaps, even, pulled over to the side of the road. But for some reason I didn't. I don't know why. Perhaps I thought I would be done in a second. Perhaps it was because no one was around, the street was deserted. Perhaps I just couldn't be bothered.

I remember the girl's face the most because she had just turned to look in my direction. She had a wonderful smile on her face. The sort of smile someone smiles when they know for an indisputable fact, deep within their heart, that someone else loves them. I remember thinking she looked as if she'd just finished kissing the man in her passenger seat. She was truly the definition of starry-eyed. But her starry eyes immediately clouded over with fear as they met my own, panicked ones and her recently kissed mouth broke open wide into a silent gasp—over which the screeching of my tyres was effectively dubbed, making it look like some sort of dodgy B-grade movie scream. She had her left hand on the wheel and her right arm hanging out the window. I saw the knuckles on her left hand turn white and I winced as I watched the front of my van ram her right arm, flattening and crunching it into her side door.

I remember the immediate thought that raced into my brain faster than one of those Japanese bullet trains: what were they doing kissing like that just before pulling out into a public road, for fuck's sake? But the sight of the ladder flying off my roof rack and towards the young girl's side window was the end of the line for that particular train of thought. Put simply, I was rendered unable to think. I was only able to watch. Watch as the ladder crashed through the side window. Watch the knuckles on the young woman's left hand turn even whiter as the ridiculously sharp, jagged ladder steps sliced through the skin, muscle, and bone of her slender neck and then straight on through the skin, muscle and bone of the slightly thicker neck of the stunned young man sitting next to her. Watch their two heads, whose combined age was less than my own, fling into the back seat of the car. Watch the remaining bodies slump forward towards the dashboard and cascade blood against the front window—which, perhaps surprisingly, was still intact—like some inside-out macabre car wash.

I don't remember getting out of my van. One minute I was sitting there and the next I was standing at the other vehicle's rear window. I was stunned. There was nothing I could do but stand there with the window winder in my hand. I stared down at it and then at the two heads lying at opposite ends of the back seat and then suddenly, in a seething fit of frustration and anger, I flung the window winder at the car as hard as I could.

'Stupid bloody thing!' I yelled. 'You stupid bloody thing!' At the time it seemed necessary to blame the deaths of two young people on a window winder. As the years have passed, I have learnt to accept my own responsibility. But it hasn't been easy, not by a long stretch. The truth is, I doubt whether I could have come to terms with it at all, had I not seen what I saw next. In fact, had I not seen what I saw next, I think I would have maybe just gotten straight back into my van and driven off the nearest cliff.

I must have thrown the window winder freakishly hard. It flew in through the driver's side window and smacked into the column shift gear stick just behind the steering wheel, causing the young couple's car to shift gears and roll ever so slightly back from the twist of bumpers and crash metal. That car must have rolled about three feet. I didn't try to stop it—there was no point doing anything and I was still too shocked to think clearly. I stood and watched it roll slowly into the slight dip between the road and the carpark. I happened to be looking right through the back window and I gasped as I realised I was staring at the young lady's head on the back seat and then I gasped again as I realised that she was actually staring right back at me. I couldn't take my eyes off hers and I swear she was looking at me as if to say: what were you doing reaching for a dropped window winder while you sped down a public road for fuck's sake?

I also swear that what happened next is true.

There hasn't been an overwhelming amount of research done on how long a human can retain consciousness after decapitation. There aren't a lot of research volunteers, as you can imagine. I remember reading once that a guillotined head managed to wink nearly thirty seconds after it landed on a linoleum execution floor, as an agreed sign to a curious doctor that the decapitated mind was still active. I don't know exactly how long it was between the time the ladder went through the window and the time I was standing watching as the car rolled backwards into the dip. It could have been ten seconds or it could have been ten minutes. I haven't a clue. I was in shock. All I know is this: as the car slipped into the dip, it rocked back gently and settled. This gentle, yet sudden rock, seemed to be all the impetus the young lady needed.

I could see the strained look on her face and the desperation in her eyes as she willed her head to roll along the back seat, closer to her lover's. And then somehow, ever so slowly and awkwardly, it did. I had that sinking feeling you get when you play pool and you've ever so gently nudged the eight-ball over to the pocket and it's slowing down as it approaches the lip and you're hoping it's going to keep moving for that last millimetre and drop, but in your heart you know it won't. In my heart I knew her head wouldn't roll all the way across the seat. But fortunately, hearts can be wrong.

Not only did the young girl's head reach her lover's, but they managed to end up noses pressed against each other's cheeks. I couldn't see the look on the man's face but seeing the look in that girl's eyes was as close as I reckon a person can get to actually seeing love itself. I stood back, eager not to intrude on their final moment together, but I was unable to look away completely. It was too fascinating. The two heads were pouring tears out as fast as their necks were dripping blood. I think I saw the girl mouth the words 'I love you' but I couldn't be sure because my own eyes were welling up and it could have just been her last gasps of breath. One thing I can be sure of is that what happened next was a conscious decision between the two heads. I've never been surer of anything else in my life.

Gently, yet firmly, they manoeuvred their lips from each other cheeks to each other's mouths. It was as if they simultaneously decided to leave life together, with a last kiss. But it wasn't just a pressing of lips between two severed heads. It was a kiss that could have been the model for all kisses. A greater kiss than any screen kiss, than any first kiss, than any kiss of any two people in the history of humankind. Not only their eyes were locked. Every muscle on their draining faces seemed to have the final mission of making the kiss work. And work it did. For a good few seconds, those two kids would have outkissed any couple in any car in any Lovers Lane in the whole world. And then, the last blood drained from their necks and the last air left their brains and the kiss stopped.

I reached for my mobile phone. Obviously, I would only bother calling the police. When I'd hung up and wiped my eyes I decided to take one last look at the couple's car.

I peered in through the front window at the bodies of the young couple but I could only hold my gaze for a few seconds before I had to turn away again. It was too much. I headed back to survey the damage on my own vehicle. But I stopped. Stopped dead, in fact. Because I had to go back and see something. To see whether my eyes had deceived me. And so I went back, to find that they hadn't. There in the front seat, the bodies of the two young people were slumped, still bleeding—only less furiously—against the front windscreen.

The thing that freaked me out though, the thing I can never forget to this very day, the thing that still keeps me awake all night sometimes, is that the two of them were holding hands. 'Come on', I hear you say. 'That's not so strange. Their muscles probably just seized up at the point of death and locked together.' But here's the thing. I distinctly remember—and I think I told you before—that I smashed the girl's right hand into the side of her car with my van. And that at the time of the crash, in fact right up until the time of her decapitation, she had been gripping the steering wheel with her white-knuckled left hand. There is simply no other way to explain the fact that those bodies were holding hands other than to say that these were two rare people whose love for each other was so strong during life that they were able to physically reach out for each other even after their brains had been separated from their bodies.

And so whenever I think about life and death and beauty and tragedy, I know now that they are all forever entwined. Sometimes you just have to take what life gives you and try to remember that it is possible to find beauty in the worst tragedy. And I remind myself of three important things. One: the human mind is capable of really amazing things.

Two: there is love after death. Three: electric windows are a good idea.

---

**Stefan Laszczuk** finished his PhD in Creative Writing at University of Adelaide in 2009. He won the Australian Vogel Award in 2007 for his novel *I Dream of Magda* and the SA Premier's Literature Award in 2004 for his novel *The Goddamn Bus of Happiness.* He has also published a book of short stories called *The New Cage,* and is currently working on two further projects.

# Triangles, Squares and Circles

Ruby Ewens

## PART 1. THE SQUARE.

Separated. On their bed. In a room. Husband and wife. Like a picture. A hard, humourless day. The room is cream-yellow but smells like potpourri lavender. He puts up with it because he is a good husband, and that is what they do. Sometimes she will turn a tea-towel around her hands, over and over and over again until her fingers are bone-white. He won't notice this. But the smell of lavender sticks to the back of his throat. The burn travels from his nose up to his temple and into his lower cerebrum. A headache erupts. He remembers his father once justifying marriage. 'Commitment,' is the word he used—one word for many years of effort. Her head is buried between Poe and Garner. He watches her read but nothing really registers. He can look at her and think nothing. He doesn't need to think about these things. She is his wife and that is it, really. Beauty, commitment, sexuality, happiness, connection, intelligence...these things don't hold weight. What is there to think about? He reads the title of the story she is eating feverishly: *The Life of Art.*

'Good book?'

'Yes, actually.' My life and art, she thinks. She thrives on poetic irony.

His writing is still like a child's scrawl and her red pen stabs his ego. She edits his proofs faithfully, giving him neat circular corrections that he goes over and over again with great deliberation, brow furrowed and deep. She watches him working and feels an ache. It is an ache of longing, of things unsatisfied, of glasses tipped to the edge of half-empty, not half-full. His hands are not like most men she sees. They are buttery, smooth, relaxed. There are no knots tying him to his work, no knobbly bits, no brown rusted marks showing where he nailed or screwed or hammered. They are supple, like a woman's. She would love to render them in an oil paint. He is her husband: the man she chose over all others. At what point did she not need anything else? Surprisingly, it is not when she reads the works of wonderful writers that harness words full of feeling and purpose that she understands the geometry of relationships. No, it is only when she is reading his engineering papers that she sees people played out in patterns and shapes. Married couples are like perfectly formed squares. They have four sides fencing them in, holding them into a box. Sometimes they think beyond the square, but sometimes they are simply the square itself: contained, straight-edged, equal, finite and predictable.

She watches him and a million thoughts come to mind: his laugh, that look of concentration that makes her thighs tighten, his thin pursed lips like a simple red line. These are the things that connect them together now—no longer those lustful thoughts she once had when they first met (the throb of a fattening vein, the glistening drop on the tip, the shiver in her ribs under his fingers). She compared him once to her other lovers. She could count how many people she had been with on one hand and he was never the best lover she had known. Others had made her grip the bed like she was fighting a pulling tide, desperate but resistant to get swept away on the ecstatic flotsam. Others had nurtured her creative side, pulling the threads of her wild ideas and weaving them into something brilliantly raw. But it was simple: she had fallen, or stayed with him, because he was faithful. Because he showed her dedication in the places no other man had offered. He never scolded her when she was sulky or sullen, he never ran away when she felt like she was losing control. He tucked her into him, smoothed her down and made her feel like everything was going to be okay.

'Good job?' she asks him.

'Yes, it is,' he nods slowly. Affection oozes out of her, but runs away from him. She hopes, if one day it is all over and done with, if she ever had the courage to walk away, she will still remember his kindness. He draws lines in all directions: boxed squares, sharp triangles, grids and diagrams. He can see the bigger picture—see exactly how those lines will feel, look, become. She sighs, which triggers a curious look from him. She smiles and his eyes return to the wide, crisp sheets.

## PART 2. THE TRIANGLE.

She remembers hearing the sentence before, so many times now that it could almost be classified as a cliché: 'it should never have happened.' She's familiar with betrayal, with abandonment. His attention is sudden and extreme and she is certain it will wane like all the other men she has known. She wishes she could remember the moment they were connected, but she can't. Maybe it was an email at work somewhere, a joke—something not only funny, but moving. He is persistent: he didn't know she was married. She doesn't understand the place she is in and therefore cannot explain it to him. He listens so intently that she finds herself opening up like a clam, ready to show him her pink, delicate parts. She knows men take this aphrodisiac for granted: the simple act of offering a space women can plug their private thoughts into. Just to listen to her. He spends most of his time outside on inspections so when she occasionally spots him she blushes, flushed by a sudden rush of hormone and not knowing what to do with the tingling sensation on her tongue. She feels his clear, blue eyes undress her. She imagines him pushing her against the wall, riding up her work skirt with his large hands, his tongue entering her at some point. The daydreams get dirtier and more intense. She tries to concentrate on the conversations they have. She notices his hands. They are sunburnt, laboured, scarred, roughened. They have rusted spots revealing intimate details where he nailed, screwed and hammered. She thinks of them on her skin, that sensation of scouring: the meeting of soft and hard. She shivers at the thought of it. They meet in those in-between moments: quiet little slices of time, not allocated to anything or anyone in particular, where they are allowed to fruit and ripen. Then suddenly, like an explosion, she finds her heart tearing at the sight of him. She understands now: she is no longer in a square, just her husband and her; she is metamorphosing into the shape of a triangle. It is a scalene triangle and she is the hypotenuse: they come together and go apart, always meeting at the centre. She has two men at either angle—neither admirable in their fight for her, but both as demanding.

They begin to have coffee in corners. He kisses her and she recoils at such a public show of affection. He goes to hold her hand and she refuses him unless it is pitch-black and he is bringing her attention to the starry-sky while they walk to the bus stop and she doesn't notice his large hand slipping over hers as they go back to what she once knew as reality. She feels this definition is necessary: it is not wrong, because he is not *real.* He will disappear as quickly and muffled as he appeared.

'I'm not judging you, but sooner or later you'll have to choose,' he says. She watches them: his lips. Her desire to kiss them wanes with his words. She wants to shut them, bandage them tight in masking tape until he is mummified with her denial.

'And yet I feel like I'm being judged.'

'I'm sorry,' he retraces, 'no, I'm not judging. We can't...I can't keep doing this. I want everyone to know.'

She hasn't thought about this: the idea of it being *more.* How could it ever be more than it is? It is already much more than she had wanted. She has been lying to her husband for a long time now about where she had been, who she had been with. As if he no longer knew her: he was just a flatmate she went to bed with.

'I love you,' she says. She regrets it immediately. He is the mirror she looks into every morning: the regret, the guilt, the self-loathing. Is it just lust? Is she even capable of love anymore? Why would anyone want to love *her?* 'But it's more complicated than that,' she concludes.

'Then I have to stop.' Lips suddenly like a tight-rope. She feels like she could walk along this line he creates for her, but the possibility of falling off is high. She reaches out and runs her thumb along his chin. She cannot help but think of her husband: upon her with slow, methodical thrusts that leave her bone dry and tasteless. But then she flinches as she recalls his overwhelming care with her clothes, the gentleness that he provokes, unlike the man sitting in front of her. He bows, kissing her palm.

'Just give me one more night,' he pleads as she shakes her head. 'Give me a morning with you. Only once.'

## PART 3. THE CIRCLE.

She isn't playing the role of the good wife properly. She is being a slack actress. She can't even find the right words to say. How many glasses had she had? The bubbles of champagne are running up to her head, fusing together. It is like she is looking at the scene from a distance: outside herself she sees the cruelty in the play, the drama in her actions and she just wants it all to stop. She wants to say: *'I'm sorry I will hurt you. I'm so sorry.'* Instead she tells him she doesn't love him anymore. Broken parts of her bobbing like bottles on a wide, gaping ocean. He watches her with flighty eyes: confused at what she is saying and even more at *why* she is saying it. He is her *husband* for god's sake. His vicious words masked by politeness hit her harder than stones. *Not here,* is what his eyes say. She hates him so much she uses all her energy not to lash out and scratch his face. She wants him to be someone else. She will never be able to feel the same way again. They are drowning in a laughing soup: sitting in the back row of a comedy show where a young American tells jokes in front of panels of thick red velvet. *I'm so sorry,* she shudders. Waves of applause wash over them and she hears herself in the midst of it all, feeling something inside slightly crumble. The fire is going out, only slow smouldering embers left in her argument. It will all be okay, she knows. She will wake up with a headache the next morning and he will forgive her on the premise she had to lay off the wine for a while. They will blame the alcohol, bitch about the bad comedy and settle down again on opposite sides of the bed like they always did. She thinks of the night to come: she has promised twenty-four hours to another man. Her will for that white flag is fading.

✦

Inseparable. On her bed. In a room. Like a picture. Nothing needs to be said. This is the letting go. They have nurtured each other for months, feeding their desire, fattening up. They make love. She thinks time—and choices of words—are so important. She can't even use the word fuck. Or screw. Or even sex. It isn't like that, it doesn't have that nature: it has height and width and depth and diameter. It has dimensions she coils herself into, like a shell, where she can hear the outside world pass in and out like a rushing tide. But inside, it is silent and still and dark. Clouded, charred, tender. The numbness escapes her and she feels human again. *Sew me up.* She wants to sleep like a foetus arched in the chambers of his heart. For him to lick the jagged edges. In the same bed. Shredded Poe and stabbed Garner at their feet. Her head jailed between two people. She bites and slices her lip, causing them both to flinch. Tears scream down her face. He looks at her like she is the most beautiful woman on the earth in that moment. She doesn't ever remember being looked at like that and suddenly feels shy, tugging at the covers to hide from this hungry gaze. He kisses her bloody tongue, counteracting her movements, exposing her. The light is too bright, her skin is too white, she feels him move beneath her skin. Scratching. Trying to pin her down. Drinking the blood from her lips.

She is soaring inland, ascending from a wild, cold plateau. It must be morning. The curtains are beginning to glow with that faint bone pale warmth. She waits for the coffee smells, the clink of plates. The man next to her is not her husband and she wonders if she is dreaming.

He gets up without a word, puts on his clothes quickly and tucks her into the sheets:

'Thank you.'

She hears the door click shut, the engine spark and rumble. Her heart sinks at the two words and she feels flushed and confused like she is a teenager again, discarded once her service is fulfilled. Maybe he understood the situation better than she ever did. She had simply been comatosed by their affair. She realises he has always had this in his mind: not just a goodbye, but a finalisation. Somehow, he has the upper hand and she feels left behind in the story.

The pillows still hold the smell of his breath. She cannot help but replay the night back: deeper, deeper, *deeper!* Gasps... *Can I keep you?* Her hands explore the pink, warm, still sticky mound. Love will never conquer such pain. It is undulating and unrelenting. It is a circle: a beautiful round moon of conflict. Maybe she will finally become this shape: the circle. The single person. A circle cannot be any other shape: it is not a polygon. No edges. No vertices. No different sides. It is a navel-gazer. It is a lonely shape, full with the possibility, yet the absence, of romance. It never moves forward on its own: it is continually moving back in on itself.

The tart of lavender sticks to the back of her throat. She should really change the room diffuser: she can no longer live with the scent. It reminds her of lazy stale nights, marking geography papers, of husbands, of old age, of her stale angry mind. It's beginning to remind her of death. Maybe she should get up and change the sheets. The warmth of him and a pasty film of his lust glazes her skin. Maybe in a minute. She looks at her book and thinks: *the art of life.* She picks it up, rubbing at her face, realising there was something wrong when he left, the feeling of abandonment peeling off her. It wasn't his lips and the two final words, but his eyes that betrayed himself. The sorrow of his eyes will never leave her.

---

**Ruby Ewens** graduated from Adelaide University in 2010 with her Masters, working in poetry and fiction. Inspired heavily by the styles of Marquez, Garner and Winton. Still working on her Masters thesis to one day be crowned with publication. Wrote her first story aged 6 and has been writing ever since.

# Beautiful Girl

Gillian Britton

She slams Lucy's door, turning away from it just as the boys thunder past her, their huge, oblivious feet threatening the stacks of slate lining the walls outside Lucy's room. A buckled strap from one of their backpacks whips at her face and she puts a hand to her cheek, although the pain seems only dimly related to her. She watches the boys jump down the temporary metal stairs to the kitchen and is only then aware of Tom, leaning at the sink with a coffee, his eyes on her.

'She's not going to school then,' he says.

She turns back to Lucy's door.

'Mick,' Tom says.

She breathes.

'Michaela,' Tom says.

Stuck to Lucy's door with a wad of blutack is a crooked-smiled, wobble-bodied fairy she'd painted when she was only three or four. Nothing like the bloodless waifs she paints nowadays, with their dead eyes and dripping jowls. Is it a good sign, Michaela wonders, that she keeps such innocence tacked to her door?

'Mick.' Tom is standing next to her now. He has his eyes on Lucy's door too but she can't help noticing that his feet stay angled towards the kitchen and the boys. He tugs at his shirtsleeves. Michaela knows that gesture.

'Is she dressed?' he says.

'What difference does it make?' she says.

'She made an agreement to go to school today,' he says and then before Michaela can stop him he puts a fist to the door and bangs.

'Lucy,' he says, 'time to go.'

As if there is any chance Lucy will pick herself up from her puddle of self-loathing to do Tom's bidding. When it is clear that Lucy is not going to respond he makes to bang on the door again. Michaela puts a hand to his arm.

'Don't,' she says.

'Why?'

'Because it won't help,' she says.

'She has to go to school today,' he says.

'So what are you going to do?' she says. 'Put her over your shoulder and carry her?'

'If necessary.'

'Don't be absurd.' She turns away. Stares out of the vast, horribly expensive triple-glazed windows that run the length of the passage opposite the kids' bedrooms. Last night she'd stared out in exactly the same way and seen a mother fox and its litter standing motionless in the field, illuminated by the full moon. She would like to tell Tom this. She would like not to be having this endless wrangle over Lucy.

Angus yells from the kitchen. 'Dad, Stepmother, whichever of you is taking us. We're gonna miss the bus. Again. Come on.'

Tom flicks his wrist to check the time. When his eyes return to Lucy's door Michaela turns and walks away from him, rattling down the makeshift stairs to the kitchen. Both boys are by the back door, backpacks on, leaning on the Aga, which has been unceremoniously dumped there until they can afford to have it fitted. Angus is on his phone, Jamie's slurping cereal from a tipped-up bowl.

Tom, who has followed Michaela down the stairs, stands at the sink across from her. In an effort to ignore him she surveys the mess on the bench where she leans—breakfast debris, the three lunchboxes she had earlier packed for the kids, and next to them, the Barbers' file. Her eyes linger on it. Her stomach twists with anxiety.

Tom continues his reprise. 'Michaela,' he says, 'she has to go to school.'

'I know she has to go to school,' she says.

'You give in to her every time,' he shakes his head.

'So what do you suggest I do?' she says.

'Put some consequences in place…'

'Like what, Tom?'

'Make it less rewarding for her to be here…'

'What does that mean?'

'She does whatever she goddamned pleases, Mick. She paints, she reads—half the time I come home to find you both sprawled on the couch watching movies.'

'I do that to get her out of her room.'

'And in the meantime you sacrifice your own work…'

'You're not telling me anything I don't already know.'

'All I'm saying is that maybe if it was more rewarding for her to go to school than it was for her to stay home…'

'You mean I should make the one place in the world she feels safe and happy less pleasant than her worst nightmare…'

The volume is getting louder, the tone more desperate.

'You have to go to work today, Mick,' he says.

She yells at him then. 'I thought we were talking about Lucy!'

'We are,' he yells back. And then he puts his hands to his face. Takes them away again to say, 'I'm sorry.' He reaches across the space to take her hand. He rubs at her fingers and says, 'It's just...'

'I know what you're going to say,' she says. 'I can't cancel the Barbers again…'

'Dad, who's taking us?' Angus says.

'Just wait, mate,' Tom says. A moment's silence follows. Angus's phone beeps. Jamie burps loudly and sets his bowl down on the Aga.

Tom has his attention fixed on Michaela. Finally he sighs. Lifts his hands and drops them in a gesture of defeat. 'So what are you going to do?' he says.

'I have no idea,' Michaela says. And then she starts to cry.

'Mick,' he says.

'Dad,' Angus says.

Tom moves to hug Michaela but she shakes her head, wards him off with raised hands. He retreats to lean on the sink with his arms crossed, staring into space. Michaela is conscious of the noise of her own snivelling. Conscious of the boys regarding her, even as they pretend to ignore her. Angus's phone beeps again. He works away at it with deft thumbs. Michaela snatches tissues from the box, reaching across the three dutifully—lovingly—packed lunchboxes. Daft hope, she thinks, and blows her nose.

'Dad,' Angus says again.

'Just go, Tom,' she says.

But he won't just go. He isn't that sort of man. Didn't she marry him precisely because he isn't that sort of man?

He changes strategy instead. 'Could your parents come up?' he says.

'Dad's just had his knee done,' she reminds him. 'Mum won't drive all the way up here on her own.'

He sighs. Says, 'I can't help—I've got meetings all day.' She listens to him hesitate before he says, 'What about Franco?'

She shakes her head.

Another pause before he says, 'He is her father, Mick…'

'I thought he was a prick,' Angus says. He looks up from

his phone to see both Tom and Michaela staring at him. 'Mick's ex-prick,' he says, 'that's what you call him, Dad, don't try and deny it.' He shoves away from the Aga then and says, 'Can we go now? Some of us actually want to go to school.'

'He could come up for a few hours, Mick,' Tom says. 'Just while you meet with the Barbers…'

'I've already tried him,' she says. 'He's not answering his phone.'

'Typical.'

'He's probably away.'

'Well, like I said. His daughter's a basket case but what the hell, surf's up in Maui. Fucking prick,' he mutters under his breath.

'Language, Dad,' Jamie says.

'And in the meantime your hard work goes nowhere,' Tom says. 'Seriously, Mick—you don't front up today and you can kiss the Barber contract goodbye. And then what do we do?' His hands rise again, that same gesture of defeat, taking in the half-finished mess of their lives. 'Of course if Franco bothered to pay his child support…' he mutters.

'He does pay it,' she says.

'He doesn't pay what he should pay,' he says, tugging at his sleeves again. She sees the muscles in his jaw clench. 'She has to go to school, Mick,' he says.

Angus joins the conversation then. 'I don't know why you bother forcing her,' he says. 'It's not like she does anything at school.'

'What do you mean?' Tom turns to him. So does Michaela.

Angus shrugs, avoids the parental spotlight by staring at his phone.

'He means, she doesn't go to classes,' Jamie says.

'What do you mean, she doesn't go to classes?' Tom says.

'She hides in the loos,' Jamie says.

'Or the library,' Angus says.

'Or the sick room,' Jamie says.

Tom looks from one to the other of his sons. 'Is that true?' he says.

'Why would we make it up?' Angus says.

Tom turns to Michaela. 'This is what we pay the astronomical school fees for,' he says. 'We're going to have to talk to the principal again. Or that useless counsellor.'

But Michaela's focus remains on the boys. 'Do you ever try to help her?' she says. 'Invite her into your group, or…'

Angus lets out a snort of laughter.

'What's funny?' Michaela says.

Angus studies his phone again. Looking up to see Michaela still staring at him, he says, 'It's not my fault. Don't start blaming me for it…'

'Nobody's blaming you, mate,' Tom says. 'But maybe you could try and help her out a bit.'

'It doesn't work like that, Dad,' Angus says. 'She's the one that's freaking out. She's the one that won't talk to anyone.'

'Are kids mean to her?' Tom asks.

'No, but it's kind of creepy so people leave her alone.' He shoves his phone in his blazer pocket and hitches his backpack up. 'Can we go?' he says.

Michaela has her head down. She's trying to pull herself together, she really is, but there's the sound of her snivelling again. Angus raises his eyes to the ceiling. Tom reaches for the car keys, which are on the bench behind Michaela. He tosses them at Angus. 'I'll be out in a minute,' he says.

'We'll miss the bus.' Angus says.

'Then I'll take you to school,' Tom says.

'I wanna catch the bus,' Jamie whines.

'Out,' Tom says. 'I'll be out in a minute.'

Michaela reaches for more tissues as the boys shuffle towards the door. 'Take your lunches,' she says, noticing their lunchboxes still on the bench.

Angus says, 'We don't eat your lunches, Stepmother, haven't you noticed?'

'Angus, take your goddamned lunch,' Tom says.

'Why can't you give us lunch money like Mum does?' Jamie whines.

Michaela, blowing her nose, looks across at Tom, who is staring at Jamie. She can read the rant about his ex-wife's financial incompetence running through his mind but, while he's happy enough to criticise Franco, he is fastidious about not slandering his ex in front of the boys. 'Take your lunch,' he says.

And so the boys drag their feet across to the bench to retrieve their lunchboxes, and in the inevitable scuffle that follows, Jamie's backpack swings around, upending an open container of milk. Michaela sees this, Tom sees this, the boys don't—they're shoving at each other, fighting over the lunchboxes, all three of which end up on the floor. Tom moves to pull the boys out of the way as Michaela hurls herself the length of the bench. Too late. She holds the Barbers' file aloft, milk dripping. Jamie lets out a snort of laughter.

She stares at him. 'I was up all night finishing this fucking thing,' she screams.

'Whoa, Stepmama,' Angus says under his breath, eyes averted. There's a moment's silence before both boys snort with laughter. She slams the file down on the bench, droplets of milk flying.

'You spoiled little shits,' she says, turning on them.

'Mick…' Tom tries to interrupt but she yells over him.

'I cook for you. I clean up your crap. I do everything I can to make things as fun and homey here as it is at your mother's but since we don't have the big screen TVs in every room and every other whizz-bang technological thing you consider absolutely essential to your health and wellbeing, you complain, don't you? Endlessly. Does it ever occur to you that we can't afford to buy these things because your father, on top of what he pays for your school fees and your sporting fees and your music tuition and your goddamned cultural visits to China, has to pay your mother, who claims she can't work because she's devoted to mothering you?'

She slaps a hand at her chest. 'I have to work so that she can have the privilege of not, do you get that?' she yells. 'And consequently while you all slept soundly in your beds last night, I was up working on this,' she slams her hand on the ruined file, 'in order to front up to the Barbers today with a spellbinding design for a house we could not afford to build for ourselves in a million years, in order to earn enough money to finish building this place which, to be perfectly frank, I have come to hate. Yes, you heard me—I hate it. It's ugly. Cold. There's not a shred of kindness in it, just like there's not a shred of kindness in you.'

The boys have their eyes cast to the floor but she knows better than to read this as shame. She feels suddenly overwhelmingly tired.

'You used to adore Lucy,' she says.

'It's not our fault,' Angus says again.

'No,' Michaela says, 'it's not your fault. It's my fault. But you don't help, you selfish little shits. You don't help at all.'

✦

'Mummy.'

Michaela has her hands over her face in the silence after they leave. She lifts them away and listens. Lucy hasn't called her Mummy in years. She hears nothing more but all the same she moves up the stairs to Lucy's door. Calling Lucy's name, she opens it. Lucy is crouched on the floor, her paintings spread out around her. Michaela feels a momentary flood of relief to see that she's got herself dressed—uniform, socks, shoes—the day is perhaps retrievable, after all.

Lucy stares up at Michaela. 'Mummy,' she says again.

In the dim light Michaela sees what she thinks is a paintbrush in Lucy's hand and paint trickling down her arms, dripping onto the ghoulish portraits. It is only as her eyes adjust that she makes out the shards of mirror across the floor. The piece of mirror Lucy grips in her hand is icicle-shaped. Lucy's eyes are frozen on Michaela; her voice is dreamy. 'It fell off the back of the door when you slammed it,' she says.

'Lucy.' Michaela drops to the floor beside her and takes the mirror from her hands. Lucy relinquishes it happily enough. She allows Michaela to turn her arms, to examine the intricate lace of cuts across the pale skin. She watches calmly as Michaela snatches a discarded towel from the bed and begins to swab, inspecting the depth of the wounds. Only when Michaela starts to sob does Lucy lose it too.

'I'm sorry, Mummy,' she wails. 'I'm sorry, I'm sorry. I got dressed and everything but…'

'It's okay,' Michaela composes herself as Lucy, waking to what she has done, begins to scream. 'It's okay,' Michaela says over and over as she wraps the towel around Lucy's arms. 'Stop, Lucy, stop,' she says, pulling her in, clutching at her, stroking at her back, feeling her thinness, the vulnerable knobs of her spine, the convulsions of her breath; that breath she knows intimately, as if it were her own. 'It's going to be okay, sweetheart,' she says. 'But we need to get you to the doctor.'

'I don't want to go to the doctor,' Lucy wails.

As Michaela clutches at her a moment longer, steeling herself to act, her eyes are drawn to a photo tacked to the wall—Lucy as a little girl, laughing, incandescent, wide eyes gulping in the world. 'Oh, my beautiful girl,' she sobs.

And then she swings into action. She pulls Lucy up from

the floor. Keeping an arm around her, she steers her from the room. Murmuring gentle encouragement she walks her down through the kitchen to the back door. Her own white shirt, carefully chosen for her meeting with the Barbers, is streaked with blood but there is no time to change it now. She grabs her bag and keys from the Aga, and then leads Lucy out across the muddy drive to the car.

Once in, Lucy huddles in the far corner of her seat, her eyes closed, her arms immobilised inside the towel. Michaela reaches to pull her seatbelt around her and strap her in. Then strapping herself in, she starts the car. They move off down the steep descent of the drive. Fog hangs from the trees. The car slips in mud. Michaela stays in low gear until they hit the road. Then she puts her foot to the accelerator. She fishtails through bends, guns it on the long straight stretch into town.

She doesn't see the fox until they are almost on it. It has already been hit. It is on its side, the row of teats visible between its legs. It lifts its head, places its front paws and strains to pull itself off the road. This is when Michaela hits it. She doesn't slow down. She reaches across to take Lucy's hand. She grips hard at it.

'My beautiful girl,' she says.

---

**Gillian Britton** completed her PhD in Creative Writing at the University of Adelaide in 2012. The novel she submitted for her PhD was runner-up for a Penguin-Varuna scholarship. She is currently working on completing this novel. She has published numerous stories, most recently in *Meanjin, Island,* and *Wet Ink.*

# The Beholders

## Sean Williams

My aunt tells me a story about a friend of hers who belonged to a group called The Beholders. They weren't a clique or a cult or anything like that. They didn't even start out to become anything at all. They had only one thing in common, which was their vanity.

My aunt's friend—let's call him Art—wanted to look more beautiful. It wasn't as though he was ugly or deformed. He was in fact quite handsome. But he wasn't happy and he didn't consider plastic surgery for fears of looking like someone else. He just wanted to be himself, only better.

So he pursued...other channels. This was in the early days of d-mat, when matter transmission was even more tightly regulated than it is now. People were still worried that a machine designed to take you apart and put you back together somewhere else would result in a world of freaks and giant flies or whatever. But there's always someone who'll break the rules, if you look hard enough.

Art heard of a guy who specialised in making people beautiful. His trick was not to do it all at once: imagine if someone walked into a booth ugly and came out a super-model—the peacekeepers would be on her in a second! This guy had a system hack that would slowly improve you, bit by bit, and keep you that way, one hundred percent guaranteed.

All you had to do was install it in your home booth and let it do its job.

Art looked carefully for a downside. There didn't seem to be one. And in a world without money, who looks for the price anymore?

The hack installed smoothly and went straight to work. Art went through the first time with some trepidation, but nothing appeared to go wrong. Or right. The hacker had explained that it would take time. He would have to be patient.

Art spent a lot of hours in front of the mirror in the coming weeks, checking for changes. Slowly but surely, he began to notice a difference. Slowly but surely, he became more beautiful, exactly as he had desired.

The story could have ended there, except vanity is a spectator sport. It wasn't enough for Art alone to notice. Everybody else had to notice, too. Only they weren't noticing. No one commented on his increasing good looks. No one complimented him on his improved complexion, the new definition of his jaw, the subtly changing textures of his hair. No one said anything at all.

Perhaps they were jealous, he thought. That had to be it. It was simply impossible that they hadn't *seen.* Art resolved to wait until his beauty was such that it was almost painful to look at, at which point surely they had to say something.

A full year passed in silence. The only time anyone ever referred to his looks was a passing remark from an old rival on how his usually impeccable façade seemed to be slipping. Art put that down to nastiness, but it sowed a seed of doubt that grew and grew until finally, in something very close to desperation, he confronted two of his closest friends. Why hadn't they complimented him? Were they withholding out of spite, or something else entirely?

The answer was not one he wanted to hear. His friends had been silent purely out of embarrassment. Far from thinking that Art was getting more beautiful, they agreed with his old rival that he was letting himself go. Art had never looked older, they said. The word *shabby* was used.

Aghast, Art confronted himself in the mirror for the thousandth time, but could see no evidence of what they said. His friends looked with him, defending their absurd proposition. That new mole, he said, pointing. How can you say that is ugly? It's an age spot, they replied. That new highlight? Grey hairs. That character line? A wrinkle.

Finally, he had to believe them, even though his eyes told them that every word was a lie. They were his closest friends. They would never deceive him about something as important as this.

If he had been lied to, it was by the hacker who had made him this way.

With the help of brain scans and a series of discreet neurologists, Art was able to find out what had been done to him. The hack worked on a specific area in the brain, changing it just once, the first time he used it. The change was simple, affecting his self-image. His brain had been rewired to misinterpret any physical change as evidence of increased beauty. A bruise? A blush. Morning hair? Très chic. He could scour his face completely off with sandpaper and regard it only as an improvement. He had no choice. When Art looked at himself now, what he saw bore no relation to reality.

And there was nothing he could do about it, not legally. Changing brains is about the most illegal thing you can do, and any further change risked further damage. Art was stuck with it. But that didn't mean he resigned himself to his fate. Oh no.

With the help of his friends, Art quickly found other victims—people who had been promised increasing beauty only to find that what had changed was not their faces, but their minds. They formed a support group called The

Beholders. Their mission was simple: to get revenge. The hacker banked on the time it took for his terrible prank to reach fruition allowing him to cover his tracks. He didn't factor in the will of this many angry people and the resources they could gather between them.

The Beholders were patient and methodical. They sent out feelers. They laid traps. And eventually, they got their man.

They could have killed him, but they didn't. They didn't even confront him. Instead, they hacked him in turn, without him knowing. Now, every time he used a booth, his own sense of self altered slightly, turning him, slowly but surely, in his eyes, into a hideous freak.

Six months later, he was dead by his own hand.

You might be wondering: Why did they torment him instead of asking for him to undo the damage? If anyone could set things right, it would be him, right?

Right, but wrong. You see, in the time The Beholders had taken to catch the hacker, they had realised something very important. They were all getting older, like everyone else, no matter how they try to cheat. We will all sag and lose our looks. We will all shrink and fade away. But The Beholders will never stop thinking that they're beautiful.

If only we all could be so lucky.

---

**Sean Williams** is the author of forty novels, ninety published short stories and the occasional poem. His work has won awards, debuted at #1 on the *New York Times* hardback bestseller list, and been translated into numerous languages. In 2013 he received a PhD in Creative Writing from the University of Adelaide, where he remains a Visiting Research Fellow and an Affiliate of the J.M. Coetzee Centre for Creative Practice. This story is set in the same world as his Twinmaker series, created as part of his thesis.

# O Lucky Man

Lesley Beasley

Richard parked the car and flexed the few muscles he had left. Soon he wouldn't be able to do this. His back hurt, and his shoulders. His right leg was cramped from two hours on the accelerator. The glands under his neck were throbbing—a sure sign that he had overdone it. He massaged them gently while he surveyed the beach. It looked cold and windy, and irresistibly wild. He reached into the back seat for his scarf. If this was the last time, he would make the most of it.

It was raining by the time he reached the sand, but he didn't care. There was a shelter of sorts—four old posts covered by half a tin roof, some rusty relic from a pre-tourist era. First he stood under it, shaking the water off his jacket, his hat, his hair. Then he sat down, and finally lay back against the remains of a child's sandcastle. It wasn't too bad. With his jacket back on, done up to the neck, hat keeping the wind out, it wasn't as cold as he expected.

And at least it was different. At least there was space. He could gaze out at the rain-speckled water, at the rocks, at the waves rushing in and streaming out, and at the blurred horizon beyond the point.

It's bad for the brain, he decided, to have your line of vision cut short, especially by the walls and ceiling of a one bedroom flat. One more day would have driven him crazy.

Look to the left—the dunny door. Look to the right—a row of cupboards. Straight ahead—wow—a window looking onto a wall.

Whereas here—he sat up and clasped his knees—here, you could feel your brain expand. And no way was he going to waste a minute of it. He hadn't driven 300ks to sit in a beach house listening to tapes brought for the car.

✦

Liliana, pushing sixty, slightly arthritic and filled with bad grace, was sitting on the couch with her feet on a coffee table and a coffee going cold on the floor. She stared out at the rain, cursing Chopin with a force to match the pianist's fingers. Not that she didn't like Chopin. On the way down, driving through gum trees and farmland and country towns, she had enjoyed every note. But this was day three. She had enjoyed every note six times now. And still there was no break in the weather. It hardly seemed worth getting up each day. In fact, today she hadn't. She was still in the old track suit that did for a dressing gown. Her grey hair was sticking out at all the wrong angles. She hadn't cleaned her teeth. She hadn't had breakfast. That's what holidays were for. Getting up late, lounging around, listening to Chopin. Watching the world go by. Wishing you were younger and mornings were longer.

She stood up, stretched, and more out of habit than any real need, started her morning exercises. At sixty you couldn't be too careful. Look at Hans. One minute they had been playing golf, the next he was dead. A classic case, the doctor said. Too much of the good life and not enough exercise. If they'd walked that course instead of riding a buggy maybe he'd still be here today.

The thought stopped her in mid-stretch. She wasn't sure

she'd want that. It had been a long time and she'd built a new life—a good life. She hadn't played golf in ten years. She had cancelled all those journals he never read. She had sold the fishing gear and that damned boat he loved so much.

She had sold the business, for God's sake. Hans would have had another heart attack if he knew that, but it had been a good move. There was no money in factories now. It was cheaper to import everything. And she'd made good investments. Charlie Masters was a good stock broker—a rotten golfer, thank God, but a good broker. He had steered her through the crash with barely a scratch. The children had worried themselves sick. They kept urging her to hold on, but Charlie said no, this is the big one, sell now and buy back cheap. And he'd been right. He'd been right about a lot of things.

Flexing a long thin arm she noticed a new age spot with irritation. At least Hans didn't have to age. And he didn't have to watch her do it either. If he could walk through the door right now, he'd probably take fright and turn around. Ten years is a long time in looks after fifty. And she was missing a breast. What would he think of that? Here I am Hans, here I am darling...just let me get rid of this silicon. No, Hans wouldn't want to come back. And she wouldn't want him to either.

She wandered to the window. The beach looked great. The waves rougher than usual, way above the normal high tide mark, rushing up to the sand to reclaim debris that had been safe for months, the rocks dissolving into foam then emerging unscathed. Not a soul around except for a bird flying with the wind and a man watching the waves from the old hut. He was a young man she thought, by the look of him. A lucky man, she said to herself, no arthritis, no heart attacks. I spare you them all, she pronounced grandly, waving an imaginary wand. I give you wealth and health and a happy life. I give you love. And with a final theatrical flourish—I give you eternal youth.

✦

Richard was unaware of the blessings bestowed on him. The wind had changed and was driving rain under his shelter. His shoulders still ached from driving. When he shrugged to ease the pain, water ran down his neck. The wetter he got the less he enjoyed the view. He was cold after all. It was time to leave. He pulled the sodden hat down over his eyes, hunched his sore shoulders against the rain, and ran for the car.

---

**Lesley Beasley** completed her Masters in Creative Writing at the University of Adelaide in 2006. She has been a book reviewer for the *Canberra Times, The Age* and *Australian Book Review,* but is now beavering away at novels and Australian history. She has been shortlisted for the SA Unpublished Manuscript Award and has had stories and poetry in various small magazines.

# A Simple Matter of Aesthetics

Rebekah Clarkson

Bob was a man people called a bloke: 'Yeah. He's a good bloke, Bob.' Some might say 'salt of the earth'. Frances had a sense of this about Bob, in the same way she might sense that a child is loved. But after she has driven the length of Huon Close, circled the cul de sac and nosed her champagne Yaris into her yet to be paved driveway, she will definitively not share this view. Frances will see the finial.

In front of her, his back turned, Bob angles tools into a wheelbarrow. The man, his tools and his wheelbarrow are lightly coated in the fatigued patina of dust and dried cement, layer upon layer, accumulated over years together in the building industry.

Frances sits in her Yaris at the top of the driveway, ensconced in cream faux leather upholstery, and casts her eyes upward from Bob to the apex of the gable.

Yes, the finial is still there. Her eyes narrow. Her heart picks up speed. In a back recess of her mind she thinks: *accelerando* and also, *piu mosso.* Phantom ants march up her neck and sting into her hairline. She gets out of the car, threads her arm through the handle of her handbag and tucks it under an elbow. Slides hands down the sides of her small but shapely thighs, smoothes her navy crepe pants from Jacqui-E. Her pelvis thrusts forward as she navigates the stupidly steep driveway. She steels herself from the mental image of her beloved baby grand being winched down this slope on moving day. She reminds herself: flat blocks were much too expensive.

She had discussed the finial with Bob on Tuesday. It was her one and only—her only—modification to the Cab Sav courtyard home. No finial, just like the Sorrento, except it's the Cab Sav. Stipulated in her contract. Straightforward. Bob had nodded several times but said that in his opinion the Cab Sav looked better with the finial. He said the Cab Sav was *designed* to have the finial. Frances was surprised that Bob had had such a strong opinion; he was just the builder for god's sake. That may well be, Frances had said, but I don't want the finial, so it needs to be taken off, whatever it takes. He'd nodded again. He'd said: Right, which Frances naturally took to mean, Right, I'll do it.

People usually made much more demanding modifications, and Frances knew it. If she'd chosen the simpler Sorrento, she'd have had to change the whole lounge/dine/kitchen configuration to achieve her piano wall. It wasn't just about avoiding the drafts. Frances knew that if you opened the lid toward the right wall, you got to hear the big sound right from the piano stool and that's what she wanted. In the new piano room she even believed she could do away with monitoring water levels on the dehumidifier. Probably, she'd no longer need the humidifier. In this one room, Frances was having hardwood floorboards installed. Floorboards, to enhance the subtle, mellow voice of her Kawai.

Surely it was easier to build the Cab Sav sans finial?

✦

'Bob.'

Bob turns and crosses his arms over his broad squat chest, stretching to tuck his fingertips under his armpits. Frances thinks of footballers' photographs.

He lifts his eyebrows.

'Bob. The finial. It's still there.' Frances points to the roof, wobbles slightly as the small heel of her court shoe slips across a large piece of gravel. Later, she will find a gash in the patent leather. Her eyes cast sideways to the waiting pallet of sandstone pavers and she feels a rush of impatience, akin to the sensation of a bucket of tepid water poured over her head.

'Uh huh.' Bob turns to pick up the handles of the wheelbarrow.

'Right.' Her eyes widen. 'Okay.' She drawls the 'okay' sideways, wondering what approach to take, even though she knows that Bob isn't listening. She thinks: *ad libitum.* She must be diplomatic. Stay on his good side.

She remembers the conversation with Warwick and the other doctors and their partners the night before.

'You don't want to piss off your builder,' Warwick had said. 'You absolutely need to stay on his good side.'

'Hear, hear,' said Tim. His wife Louise lifted her glass in agreement, pursed her lips into a small smile toward Frances and took a sip. Brenton said, 'Absolutely' and Cassie, his new partner, a blonde agency nurse, murmured 'Absolutely' right on its heels. Brenton: 'For god's sake, make him a batch of your raspberry and white chocolate muffins.' Laughing and more wine. Warwick draped his arm around Frances's chair and stroked his fingertips back and forth across the round of her shoulder. Irritating, but she laughed with the others.

Tim had asked what she had against finials. 'She thinks they're daggy—architecturally inappropriate,' Warwick had answered. 'She wants her house to be *honest*—architecturally honest.' When he said 'architecturally,' he spelt out all the separate sounds of the word as though he were riding it like a rollercoaster. He squeezed Frances's shoulder, pulling her into his armpit. She smiled and shrugged, shook her head to try and free the hairs that had become caught under Warwick's jacket and were pulling against her scalp.

Tim: 'Hey! Maybe this is the *fourth dimension*—you know.' He intimated quotation marks around his ears when he said 'fourth dimension'. 'You know—emotion in architecture? Like the finial is bringing up something from your childhood.' Smiles and silence. Tim again: 'Aren't they supposed to deter witches on broomsticks from landing on your roof? Finials? Sure you don't want one, Frances?' More laughing.

She already knew this. She'd looked it up on Wikipedia at work. The doctors had recently paid for a new reception desk and the configuration of desk, return, computer and switchboard meant that she could now look at her screen without patients seeing it as well—a definite improvement. Yes, she'd thought. Finials are for fairy tales.

'Look,' she said to the amused dinner table assembly, 'it's really no big deal. Nothing from my childhood or a former life. I just don't want it. And yes, I think they're daggy. They're so—I don't know—*try hard*. Fake. But you know, I don't really have such a big opinion of it. Not really.' Warwick raised his eyebrows, smiled and leant down to kiss the top of her head. The others continued watching. Warwick took his arm away and slid down low in his chair, stretching his long bowed legs into a human slide under the table. The two women smiled at Frances with the patience of colluding schoolgirls.

'It's just one thing I happened to change on the design,' Frances went on. 'You can basically change whatever you want.' She looked around the table. 'You've all built houses, you know how it works—people change whole rooms around for goodness sakes! Laundry here. Bathroom there. All I don't want, is one of those ridiculous finials on my roof.'

What did she want? She couldn't even articulate it. Every

time she tried, it sounded too silly in her brain to send it down into her mouth.

The three men grinned and she'd remembered that the houses they had built were originals, designed by architects, every aspect to their specification. Warwick had built his after the divorce, using the same architect as Tim and Louise. He wanted Frances to move in with him. He'd said, 'You know you're more than welcome to just move in here with me.' Brenton and Cassie were renting in the city, in the interim, while Brenton's wife stayed in their five-bedroom split-level house with their kids. Frances hadn't seen Karen since the split. It had dawned on her only then, that Karen, with whom she had got along quite well, had shared dinners and bottles of wine and cups of coffee, even the odd weekend away, was no longer part of her life.

✦

Maybe it's not even the finial, Frances thinks now. Bob has turned his back on her and is wheeling his load of tools around to the back of the house. She follows him in a half trot. The cuffs of her pants skim and collect pigeon lime. Maybe it's some symbolic phallic thing, she thinks. Maybe she has a problem with men. Maybe this is why she hasn't married, why none of her relationships have lasted more than three years. She's thirty-five, for god's sake. Maybe she needs counselling.

No, Frances thinks; it is a simple matter of aesthetics. And they are *her* aesthetics.

She couldn't describe what she wanted with words, but she *felt* it whenever she played herself Tchaikovsky. And then she'd sit on the piano stool and wonder how she came to be a thirty-five year old single medical receptionist living in this town and building in Gladeville Park estate.

Anyway, she wasn't entirely single. There was Warwick.

✦

Her arm scrapes against brick as she takes the corner of her new house too quickly, pilling her cream blouse. She checks her watch. 12:15. A half hour lunch break barely gave you time to buy something to eat.

'Ah, excuse me. Bob?'

Bob continues walking until he reaches the back of the house and then sets down the wheelbarrow. He turns to face her, resuming the footballers' photograph pose. He has leathery skin from a lifetime under the Australian sun, creviced, creased and mottled with shadows. Thin strips of grey and black hair sweep across his scalp. Sideburns like unused balls of steel wool. Hard to pick, but Frances guesses early fifties. She tries to imagine that a woman might find him attractive. He lifts his stubbled chin at her in a quick motion, which Frances reads as: Speak. She takes a small step backwards.

'Look. Maybe you haven't got to it yet, but…well, I'm just checking on the finial. Look, everything else is fine. It's fine.' She gestures with her hand; up, down and around. 'But, I'd like to know when you are going to remove the finial, please.' She thinks of Warwick with the please. Bob squints his eyes, sharpens his mouth into a point and takes it to one side, drops his head further into his neck.

Frances's right foot involuntarily rises an inch and stamps back down. She places the palms of her hands firmly on her thighs.

'Look. Bob. I have a stipulation in my contract.' She already went through this on Tuesday, but she does it again, this time more slowly, a conscious effort at lightheartedness. 'The contract says that the only modification I want on this house design, is that I don't want the finial. Okay, you have put the finial on the roof, the gable, the whatever, which was wrong, a mistake. So, you need to take it off. I'm sorry if that is a pain for you but it's in my contract. I'd just like to know when you are going to do it. Please.'

'Won't look right.' Bob shakes his head back and forth, like a toddler shoring up for a tantrum. 'The Cab Sav needs the finial. It's part of the *design.'* He emphasises the 'd' and rocks forward onto his toes and then back down to his heels.

Frances looks about her for sympathy from an equally bewildered but imaginary audience.

'Listen. Bob.' She says his name as if she's trying to pounce on it. 'I'm sorry. Look. It doesn't matter if it's part of the design or not. Everything is part of the *design*. The thing is, I'm changing it. And if it doesn't look right, then it's my fault. Because it's...it's, well it's actually my house. Okay?'

'No.'

'No, what?' She takes a step toward him with a sudden exhalation of breath. *Staccato:* 'Do you not agree that this is my house?'

'I won't change it. Won't look right. Sorry. Can't do it. Look, yer chose the Cab Sav, so obviously yer like the *style* of the house. The finial is part of the style of it. Yer would've been more than welcome to change the interior around. But no. No, yer can't change the *integrity* of the design.' He pauses and then lifts and sharpens his eyes with the look of a person who has just solved the final clue to a deep mystery. His voice drops, softer— 'No one has ever wanted me to leave off the finial. Everyone wants the finial. It's part of it—part of the Cab Sav. Yer don't *want* the Cab Sav without the finial.'

'Bob, but I do want the Cab Sav, because I've got it!' Frances throws an arm skyward. Gravity flops it heavily back down. She's yelling now, her heart galloping into her throat. 'And you have to take it off because I don't want it! I don't want the finial! And I'm paying you, paying you with money. I'm paying for this house and you are the builder who is getting my money. So, basically, take the finial off now! Please!'

Later, she will sit in the new IKEA arm chair in her rented unit, dabbing Dettol and cotton wool at the cuts on her hands, wincing, mentally rephrasing these last words until they sing, until they are compelling enough, she imagines, to be delivered in a film, or printed in a book. She will also kick her shoes off and notice the slash down the leather of one heel.

Bob rubs his chin, turns and picks up the wheelbarrow. Starts to walk away from her.

'Excuse me!' Frances's voice cracks in a shriek. 'I… I… well, I'll just have to call Kate at Marshall Thompson. This is…this is outrageous! You are…' Adjectives and insults tumble and vie for her selection but she can't settle on one that is up to the task. She fumbles in her bag for her phone. She holds it in her hand, which she sees is shaking. She wonders about calling Warwick first, whether he might come down and talk to Bob. That man-to-man thing. She exhales sharply. This is meant to be her house. That she owns. It would not just be humiliating to call Warwick, it would be pathetic. She's sure Kate's number is in her phone. She steadies her thumb to scroll down her contacts. Karen is before Kate. She liked Karen. They got along well. Perhaps she needed a friend to give her some perspective, some on-the-spot advice.

A phone rings, but it's not the one she's holding. A loud old-fashioned ring. Bob fumbles in the bib pocket of his khaki overalls stretched tight across his large barrelled rib cage. He pulls out a thick black phone encased in a baggy pouch. He holds it first in front of his face and then extends his arm fully and leans his head back, squinting at it. The continuing ring is so obtrusive that Frances is compelled to pause from her own task, like someone might if a freight train were passing.

'Bob.' He grunts his name into the phone but then his face softens.

'Son. Yes, son.' He nods quietly. 'You were there? Mish?' Nods again. 'Okay. Right then. Right then. I didn't think it would be today. Right then. I'll see you directly.'

Bob walks to the back wall of Frances's house and places a palm against the bricks. It took her a whole month to choose the russet of Old Red Sandstock over Sapphire. Bob drops his head for a moment and Frances wonders if his lips might be moving.

He turns his chin up over his arm and says sideways, 'Have to go.'

'Pardon?' Frances grips her phone more tightly. She folds her arms across her stomach and watches as Bob leans over his wheelbarrow. He rearranges the wood and steel handles of the larger tools, until he is satisfied with their symmetry and order and then he picks out the large dented metal toolbox from the bottom of the tray. It looks to have been once painted blue; chips and patches of colour remain on the top and sides. Frances stares at it and imagines the toolbox in a trendy shabby chic shop in the city. She watches as he takes the toolbox and turns his back to angle past her. She would move, but she seems to be stuck there. As Bob turns the corner of the house, she hears herself screech his name again.

'Bob! Bob! Excuse me! Where are you going?'

Bob stops, turns slowly back and for a moment, is perfectly still. Frances watches him closely. Grey dust freckles his head and face, making him look as though he is made of stone. She sees a small black mole underneath his left eye and notices too that his eyes are a soft green.

'There you are then,' he says finally. 'She's dead.'

'What?'

'My wife. She's dead.'

'Oh.'

'Cancer.'

'Oh. I'm...well...I'm sorry.'

Bob lifts the toolbox slightly higher.

'Don't be sorry.'

Then he looks over her head and raises his voice, as if addressing a whole group of people and says, 'Forty years next Saturday.' To himself, he mutters it again, 'Forty years.' And then he turns and walks away.

Frances places her hands and face against the glass of her dining room window. Through the empty shell of her house, she catches a glimpse of Bob through the lounge window as he makes his way up the driveway, toolbox in hand. The steepness exposes a drooped shoulder she hadn't noticed before—as though he were nursing a broken collarbone. She crouches and sees his boots as they step up into his old white ute. She hears the engine start and the sound of the tyres as they spin briefly on gravel and dust and then clunk down the kerb from her yet to be landscaped front yard.

After a moment, Frances stands and walks the short distance to Bob's abandoned wheelbarrow. Gazing into the tools, something emerges in her throat, something more she might like to say to Bob, as if part of him is still here, somehow part of the tools—as if they are his extended limbs. She opens her mouth but it is a strange groan that forms, not a word or even the notion of a word. A bird lands on the steel guttering above her, its tiny feet tapping like keyboard keys, and she thinks vaguely of her unattended reception desk. She lifts a hand and touches one of the long wooden handles. Old grey oak. Her fingers run along the length of it and she marvels at how silky and smooth it is—and warm—like running her hand down the trunk of a ghost gum in summer when she was a girl. Her fingers reach the cold steel blade, which she assumes is an axe, but is in fact Bob's thirty year old mattock. Her fingers drop to the next tool, a shorter iron rod topped with a sharp steel rectangle—a wrecking bar with a hex shank, detail also unknown to Frances.

What Frances does next is difficult for her to recall later, perhaps because her actions carry no accompanying thoughts. There are no words, no interior commentary, as she separates and lifts this last tool away from the others, feels the weight of it across her shoulder blade, and makes her way to the front of her house. At no point does she think, I'll do it myself. Nor does she think, I'll find a ladder.

When she has accomplished this thought-free action, having stumbled once on a steel rung, ripped a small hole where her pant pocket meets the leg seam, and cut her left hand badly enough that it will eventually receive three stitches, Frances lugs herself and her handbag up the driveway and sits down in the dust, resting against the front right tyre of her Yaris; it does not occur to her to sit in the car. Her eyes travel from the ground where the severed finial lies alongside the wrecking bar, up past the bricks and gutter to the apex of the gable, where the splintered base remains. A small measure of peace arrives in her chest, unforeseen and fleeting, but leaving its trace, like a stranger with a kindly voice who has rung the wrong number. It is not the peace Frances had imagined, but it is still peace. She thinks absentmindedly that this must be the longest lunch break she has ever taken in her life.

✦

Back on Wellington Road in the middle of town, noting no changes on his computer-generated patient list, Warwick bins the wrapper from his chicken salad Subway, wanders out of consulting room 3, and surveys a sea of faces in the waiting room. Yes, he thinks, Spring: flu season.

He then sees the empty ergonomic chair pushed under the reception desk. He checks his wristwatch: 3:10; glances up at the clock on the wall; pulls his mobile out of his pocket and tucks it back in. Four strides to Frances' desk. On seeing her screensaver he tilts his head, frowns, tries to make out the strange sequencing images; it looks like an old man's head in black and white, upside down and geometric, swirling and odd. The words *Bela Bartok* scroll across the bottom of the screen and Warwick wonders absentmindedly if that is the name of the man, and who he might be. He arches his long body over and hits a key to dismiss it. There isn't much more he can do. He'll just have to check the schedule himself and assume that his patient is here. He stands to his full height and straightens his tie. He sees a little pewter Eiffel Tower behind Frances' coffee mug. He didn't think she'd ever been to Europe. He finds the name of his next patient on the screen.

'Malcolm Wheeler?'

---

**Rebekah Clarkson's** short stories have been recognised in major awards, shortlists and independent publications in Australia and overseas. Most recently she was runner up in the 2013 *ABR* Elizabeth Jolley Short Story Prize and winner of the Readers' Choice Award. She has a BA in Aboriginal Studies, an MA in Creative Writing, and is currently completing a PhD at the University of Adelaide, where she also teaches.

# Duck

Bryan Whalen

I woke up at the cemetery. There was a duck next to me. I yelled at him: 'Why are you so goddamn obsessed with death?' Yelling cleared the tobacco tar from my throat, but the duck did not answer. 'It's a duck, Harold,' I said to myself. 'It's a goddamn duck.'

Below me, spread over the grass, was an orange and black, paisley-patterned sarong. Apparently, I was a well-prepared drunk—a midnight picnicker who'd found his way to Our Lady of Bethlehem. But how I had arrived there was uncertain. An empty bottle of bourbon sat beside me, covered in ants. Stuck into it, like a cork, was a rolled up piece of notebook paper. All memory of the night before was a mosaic with missing pieces. The pieces I remembered included: my ex-girlfriend playing a Jew's harp, very badly; a talking moon on my walk to the cemetery; my reflection in a windowpane, crying, what a stranger might call 'blubbering'; and a dream, a sequence of dreams.

Now it was morning.

Mourning, I was still drunk. The tombstones and the family two rows down floated in a haze. *Perhaps I am asleep,* I reasoned. Who could say? Keats. John Keats could. He said: *How can death be sleep when life is but a dream?*

I said: *Fuck you, Keats. You got me into this mess. You and Mr*

*Daniels—that dastardly Tennessean. For Christ sake, John, I read a poem at her funeral!*

What a pile. What a steaming pile of ego—as if my words were enlightened enough to memorialise *Life!* Words get you nowhere. You want to do something worthy, stay silent, become a goddamn gunslinger; become a bank robber, something out of a Tarantino movie. Let Whitman and Rilke and Charlie Bukowski rot. Let their words die with them. I'll be a mime. A drunk mime. Severely drunk. Or a monk. A drunk monk who meditates on nothingness for the rest of my goddamn life.

Alcohol sounds almost as bad as cheese. That's right, cheese is part of the mosaic: Blue and Gouda, the old Cheddar with the wax on it that my Uncle peeled with his right incisor, Brie (how I loathe the bird shit of cheese), Feta, Danish and whatnot. My family—another piece of the mosaic. What a lark! What a ruse! How pathetic.

There are goddamn ants everywhere! In Australia, there are ants that'll eat your flesh while you nap on the front lawn. But at least they're honest about their ruthlessness. The ants here, at Our Lady of Bethlehem, wait until you're dead or asleep, then steal your liquor and rape your loved ones. They're probably raping her right now. I can hear my father in the back of my mind: *They're like black people.* What a bigot. What a bogan. He laughed when I read my poem! He laughed and then sauntered out of the chapel, clapping and carrying on as if he were at the stock car races. 'Leave!' he yelled over my free verse. 'Leave your poetry in Australia. Leave! Don't ever come home.'

If I were a gunslinger, I'd have a gun; then I could get rid of this headache.

The wind is blowing the flowers from her garden hat, which I must have placed atop her tombstone last night.

Add the hat and its flowers to the mosaic: hydrangeas from the neighbour's yard, bulrush from the side of the road, tulips, lavender, rosebuds and unknowns from condolence bouquets at the wake. Oh, the wake. 'Can you eat roses?' my youngest cousin asked last night as I sipped brandy from a mason jar and stared at one of the arrangements. 'You can't eat roses,' I answered. 'They're for her, mate. We'll put them on her grave. She can enjoy their aesthetic sustenance in peace.'

He laughed. 'Mate. You just said 'mate'.'

It had been four years since I'd been in the U.S. Four years since I'd seen any of the family, except her. She visited last September, around my birthday.

'Are you speechless?' my Aunt asked me after the service. 'Aren't you just speechless, Harry?'

'Yeah,' I lied. I was about as speechless as the goddamn priest and all he had were words. Words and wine. Red wine. Communion. Symbolic goddamn cannibalism—oh how the family loves it! Alcohol, blood and meaning: our three favourite things. I wasn't speechless. Everybody just wanted me to be speechless because it was easier than talking to me. Nobody knew what to say.

Meaning. Let's hope the message in the bourbon bottle can colour our mosaic. Let's hope the lined piece of paper, blue as the firmament and smelling like hell, with more *words*, can offer us some insight.

> Home. I want to go home. It's not Australia and it isn't here. No, it's not the womb. It's not where my heart is or where my shoes are or where my stuff is. Our Lady of Bethlehem is an ocean; the headstones are lighthouses; home is this island of souls. I want to go home.

She told me, when she visited, that she loved Australia. We were sitting at a Pokie machine, at a pub across the street from my derelict apartment. She turned to me as the coins rained into the metal tray. 'Harold,' she said. She was the only person who called me by my full name. 'I love this blotty country.'

I must have looked confused, which is pretty normal. 'Bloody,' I said. 'It's bloody, ma. You love this *BLOODY* country.' We clinked glasses. 'And thank you. It bloody well loves you too.'

She scoffed. Her eyes were hard yet they were filling with tears—a beautiful contrast. I know now that she knew even then. 'It's a country, Harold. It doesn't love anybody.'

She was drunk. She was my mother.

She would have loved that goddamn duck.

---

**Bryan Whalen** has published short stories, essays and poetry in several online and print publications. In 2014 his PhD thesis in creative writing received the Dean's award for academic excellence. Born in Ventura County, California, he currently lives in Amsterdam. To read more of his work visit www.bryan-whalen.com.

# Ladies Tea Party

Lilliana Rose

Meg set her shoulders square and walked up the dozen steps. Her heart thumped a quick march as she stood in front of the looming dark wooden door. She lifted the brass handle, a lion's head with a ring in its mouth, and slammed it back down. The knock echoed deep within the Victorian mansion, causing her pulse to stammer, missing every second beat.

The door creaked open. An automaton stood in the entrance. His insides whirled and clacked as he stared at her with empty doll eyes.

'Nutmeg?' he asked, his voice a metallic tone, a deep treble, caused her insides to vibrate.

'Yes.' Hearing her code name for the tea party sent ripples along her skin.

'Please come in.' He bowed with jerky movements.

Meg stepped inside and paused at the cavernous space of the entrance. Her breath caught. Oversized windows let in the gloomy rays from the wintry day outside, oil paintings of past owners lined the wall and orange light from gas lamps warmed the space.

'Meg!' exclaimed Anise. 'How glorious it is to see you again. I'm so glad you came.' The hostess' shoulders were bare and her waist corset tight. A skirt of ruffled cream lace cascaded down from her hips, short at the front, revealing her fishnet stocking legs. Meg tried not to gape in surprise at Anise's immodesty.

'It was lovely to meet you the other week at the tea room,' said Anise as they embraced.

'Mrs Joyce makes delightful scones,' said Meg politely, unsure of the etiquette to follow.

'You should taste mine,' said Anise with a devilish smile. 'I'll have you begging for more.'

Heat rose on Meg's cheeks, colouring them a soft red. 'Well…' Her words caught in her throat. She wasn't used to such openness.

'Relax, darling.' Anise's melodic voice soothed Meg's nerves.

'Let the butler take your coat,' said Anise. 'He's an automaton for a very good reason.'

Meg unbuttoned her dark blue coat. The automaton helped her to slip her bare arms out of the sleeves. Her electric blue skirt flowed freely around her knees.

'Turn,' said Anise.

Meg spun around twice. The rich blue bustle swung out behind her.

'Stunning.' Anise smiled. 'You have great taste.'

Meg had never worn anything like this before—with so much of her skin exposed. A scandalous and delicious sensation gripped her body. This wasn't like her, but it could be.

'I've had the heating system turned on,' said Anise as she linked her arm with Meg's. 'You'll be perfectly warm.' She guided Meg into a side room where three other ladies sat on winged chairs sipping tea.

'Meet the mixed spice blend; Perilla, Clary and Dandelion.' Each lady smiled politely at Meg. 'We're still waiting for Saff. She likes to be the last to arrive.'

The hostess directed Meg to a free chair next to Perilla, who wore a long see-through skirt and a half corset over a low-cut ruffled shirt.

'That's because Saff likes to cause a scene,' said Perilla.

'Oh yes, she does like it when we are all looking at her,' said Dande. 'I wonder what delightful new clothes she will be wearing this month?'

'I can't wait to see,' said Clary. She crossed her naked legs, which were exposed due to her skirt ending mid-thigh.

'Meg you're going to have so much fun,' said Perilla. 'Won't she ladies?'

'Absolutely,' said Clary. She wore black lace gloves that reached her elbows and held her pinkie high as she sipped her tea.

'How exciting, this is your first time,' said Dande. Meg smiled, a tremor of excitement rippled within her stomach.

'Just focus on the food and everything will flow naturally,' said Anise. She handed a fresh cup of English breakfast tea to Meg, served in Royal Doulton china.

'I do enjoy new tastes,' answered Meg. Her cheeks flushed warm.

Perilla laughed. 'You will fit in beautifully.'

A knock on the front door interrupted them. 'That better be Saff,' said Anise, leaving the room.

'You look the part. Absolutely gorgeous outfit,' said Clary. 'I'm looking forward to seeing what you have underneath.'

Meg fluttered her eyelashes at Clary. 'Well now, you're just going to have to wait.'

Clary winked back. 'You're a quick learner.'

'Perilla, where did you get such patterned stockings?' asked Dande, running her hands down Perilla's legs.

'Can't say,' answered Perilla, pulling up her skirt to show off her legs.

'Darlings,' said Saff as she waltzed into the room in the rustle of her full layered dark green skirt that ended mid calf, revealing her hour-glass shaped shoes of the same colour. Her matching jacket, buttoned tight with pearls, emphasised her bust and hips.

Anise handed Saff a cup of tea. 'Meet our new guest, Nutmeg.'

'Pleasure,' said Meg.

'It's wonderful to be back with a full guest list and new blood. I can't wait to taste her,' said Saff.

Meg swallowed hard, unsure whether or not to believe the women.

'Don't worry dear, she's all talk,' said Dande. 'There's no blood.'

'If we don't eat soon I'm going to starve,' said Perilla.

'Oh you've got plenty in reserve, just use that,' said Dande.

'You're just jealous of my extra curves,' said Perilla putting her hands on her hips and wriggling, showing off her voluptuous body.

'I'm doing my best to catch up.' The ladies giggled, a polite giggle, one edged with naughtiness.

A brass bell sounded. The metallic noise settled the ladies.

'Ladies, the food is ready,' said Anise. 'This way.' Anise opened a concealed panel in the wall.

'Our newest member may have the honour,' said Anise. She motioned for Meg to come forward.

Meg ran her hands down her bodice then stepped carefully down the narrow staircase. She found herself in a low ceiling room.

A long white-clothed table stood in the centre of the room, laden with sugary delights. A three-tier fountain of chocolate stood in the middle, with a bowl of red bursting strawberries nearby.

Meg stood frozen, staring at the table. A large pavlova smothered in cream. Crystal bowls overflowing with cherries. Marshmallows scattered between plates and bowls, an innocent looking chocolate cake, bright pink and blue macaroons were arranged to make a pyramid, candy sprinkles in small jars, chocolate rum balls, truffles—white, milk and dark. The cupcakes tipped with red nipples stirred a new something inside of her.

Meg's eyes widened at the delicious sight and her mouth watered. She stepped further into the room, wanting to begin straight away.

'Mind the braziers,' warned the hostess, guiding Meg to sit down. 'We want to keep warm, not be burnt.'

Names written on ornate paper showed the women where to sit around the table. They filed into the room, gasping at the afternoon tea set out for their pleasure.

'This is amazing,' said Meg. She watched the chocolate river flow outwards, a calm waterfall of syrupy darkness tempted her to dip her fingers in and suck off the richness.

In front of each guest sat a different cupcake. Curious, Meg picked up hers; a white iced cupcake with a cherry on top.

The hostess lifted up her cupcake. 'To mixing spices.' The women each held up their cupcake in a sugary toast. Anise turned to Meg. 'How you eat your cupcake will tell us a lot about you.' Anise took a bite. Frosting squeezed out the sides of her mouth. She chewed and swallowed, her pink tongue slipped impolitely out to claim the missed delight. Her eyes rolled to white, her lids fluttered and she moaned with pleasure.

'Don't waste time.' Perilla moved her cupcake near her mouth then dragged her tongue over the top, making soft noises of sweetness.

'Some do like to make a mess,' said Clary, her voice playful as she delicately peeled away the paper of her cupcake. 'Meg, it is important to undress your food first and show some constraint.'

'Just take the biggest bite,' said Dande. She bit into her cake. Crumbs fell from her mouth, in an unladylike manner.

'No, no, no. You've got to smell it first.' said Clary.

'Just as long as you taste it properly,' said Perilla.

'And soon.' Her hostess gave Meg a gentle nudge. 'We want to know how you like to treat your food.'

'Just like this,' said Meg, lifting the cupcake, frosting side to her mouth. She flicked out her tongue and caught the fake cherry that sat on top. Saff hooted with delight. Meg sunk her teeth into the white icing and chocolate sponge, taking the biggest mouthful she could.

'You're a tease,' said Perilla.

'You know what you want,' said Dande.

'Meg, darling, welcome to our group,' said Anise.

Meg chewed the excessive mouthful. Sugar hit her taste buds in bubbles of joy. Her eyes fluttered from the rich taste, so unlike what she'd eaten before. She swallowed. 'Oh my.'

'It's the best you've tasted, isn't it?' said Dande. Chocolate staining the corners of her mouth.

'Oh yes,' said Meg. She leaned back in the chair catching her breath.

'Anise chains up her cook at night so we don't steal her,' said Clary.

'Well now, you would do the same too,' said Anise.

'Naturally,' said Clary.

'You've dropped some crumbs.' Anise sucked on her finger and dragged it out slow and wet. 'Here let me.' She pressed her moist finger on Meg's chest, picking up the chocolate crumbs and offered them to Meg, who, without hesitation, sucked off the missed crumbs, savouring the soft sweetness edged with saltiness.

'You do know how to increase the heat in here,' said Clary, standing and reaching for the strawberries. She placed her red painted lips over the belly of the strawberry and sucked while she unbuttoned her jacket, shedding a layer and revealing a black laced chemise that clung to her skin. She bit down on the strawberry. Juice spilled around her lips.

Perilla whistled.

'Now behave.' Clary winked, her hands on her hips and her chest pushed forward.

Perilla ran her finger through the flowing chocolate, dipped it in the bowl of candy sprinkles, then topped off the creation with a dollop of cream.

'Is that for me?' asked Dande.

'Well it was going to be all mine, but I don't mind sharing.' Perilla held her finger to Dande, who delicately wrapped her pink tongue over the sweetness.

'You have to try this,' said Clary. She slipped a half bitten truffle into Meg's mouth.

A burst of darkness, spiced with chilli, caused Meg to flush. 'Too hot.' Meg stood up and slowly untied her skirt, making a show of it and wriggling out of the material, showing her suspenders and tight lacy undergarments.

'I need more room.' Perilla leaned back and patted her belly.

'Need help?' Dande pulled at the cords of Perilla's corset and peeled off the layer.

'Finally I'm free,' said Perilla. She wriggled her shoulders, dancing her breasts. Tassels on her nipples swung in a provocative motion. The other ladies cheered and clapped. More clothing slipped from hot skin and swelling bodies, piling on the floor, forgotten.

'I don't know why I wear these restrictive things,' said Clary undoing the metal hooks along the front of her corset.

'You do so,' said Saff.

Clary laughed and threw her corset away. She stretched her arms above her head and wriggled her shoulders.

'Showing off again,' said Perilla.

Clary smiled. 'Only if you are.'

'I have a surprise.' Anise stood up, untied the ribbon around her waist, releasing her skirt. The material crumbled around her ankles.

'That's no surprise,' said Clary. 'Though maybe to Meg.'

'Don't get ahead of yourselves.' Anise turned and walked to the wall, swinging her hips, causing the ladies to whistle. She bent down, revealing her lacy briefs were crutch-less.

The ladies gasped.

'Is that all?' asked Saff cheekily.

'No.' Anise turned back to face the ladies, picking up a tray and holding it at chest height, six bite sized balls aligned on top. 'Ice cream.'

'I haven't had any for ages,' said Meg, her breath quick and shallow.

Anise rested the tray on the table, put her foot on the chair, rolled down her stockings then lined the balls on her thigh. 'Come on ladies before they melt, and I cool down too much.'

The ladies scrambled for a taste.

'I'll have more of that,' said Dande, licking her lips.

'Maybe next month.' Anise put her foot on the floor. 'I need to heat up again.'

'I can help you with that,' said Saff. Leaning over she ran her tongue over Anise's thigh.

'That will do it,' gasped Anise. Her head tilted backwards as she savoured the sensation rippling through her body.

'I want more,' said Meg. Her mouth watered as she lapped the remaining ice cream from her lips.

'What about this instead.' Dande pinched her backside and Meg squealed.

'Steady on,' said Dande. 'Make sounds like that and I'll have to keep pinching you.'

Meg's face flushed and she took up the challenge by blowing a kiss to Dande. Dande pinched her again and Meg shrieked.

'Chocolate, Saff?' asked Perilla, presenting her neck smeared with the dark liquid. Saff leaned over and slid her tongue over the chocolate. Perilla moaned with joy.

'There's more,' said Anise. She reached under the table and pulled out a canister with a spout and lever at the top. 'Whipped cream anyone?'

A chorus of 'yes' echoed in the room.

'There's plenty to go around.' She turned the brass hooks on the front of her corset.

'Oh, hurry up,' said Perilla.

'You take way too long,' said Dande, pausing from nibbling on Clary's ear.

'Show us your beauties,' said Saff.

With a coy expression on Anise's face she peeled away the corset and dropped it to the ground. Shining gold stars twinkled on the ends of her ample breasts.

'That's better.' Anise shook them as if bringing them back to life and sat backwards on the chair. She leaned back, held the canister up and sprayed curves of thick creamy whiteness on her chest.

'Let me clean up this mess,' said Meg. She glided her tongue over Anise's creamed skin, bitting gently. Anise gasped.

'My turn.' Clary sucked off the remaining cream. 'Hmm, cinnamon.'

'I want to see how this works,' Meg took the canister and pointed it at Dande. She pulled the lever. Cream sprayed out over Dande, who screamed with delight.

'I could get used to this.' Meg held the spout to her mouth and pressed until the cream dribbled from her mouth.

'What a great idea.' Clary grabbed the cylinder and did the same.

Meg pulled at her corset, unhooking top to bottom, freeing herself. Someone sprayed cream along her cleavage. Tongues slid over her skin, teeth nibbled for more, and her blood sugar level boiled, bubbling over into a thick burnt toffee, all moist and hot.

'Do it again,' Meg panted. More cream flowed over her. Candy sprinkles tumbled down catching on her sugared skin. Meg began to lose herself, giving herself up to the sensation of pleasure.

'Open up,' said Anise with a chocolate-coated strawberry in hand.

'I'm full,' gasped Meg.

'Just a little more.' Anise slipped the strawberry between her lips, straddled Meg, and placed their lips together. Meg opened to receive the fruit. The natural sweetness mixed with the chocolate burst onto her taste buds, hidden spices in the chocolate warmed her mouth. But it was the hint of salt that sent her tumbling over the edge.

Meg gasped. Her eyes rolled back, as the pleasure slipped down her throat, the spices bringing her body to life. Her vision blurred and the room spun around in a coloured smear of delights and skin. Her breath rapid, she held onto Anise for support, breasts hard against hers.

The other ladies came in closer. They moved together.

A tongue ran over her belly. Lips found hers. Meg tumbled off the chair; lay open on the floor, with other bodies entwined with hers. Her own hands touched and squeezed fleshy delights. Skin next to skin there were no places left untouched. Meg's back arched, her legs opened, fingers and tongues dipped into her honeyed juices as the tasting continued until she shuddered and the other women quivered and trembled with her as the sugary bliss finally burst, spilling out into the room with the delicious sounds of screams.

Satisfyingly full, completely spent, Meg lay in the sticky sweetness that held them all.

'Same time next month?' whispered Anise into her ear.

Hot breath sent Meg's skin prickling. 'I wouldn't miss it.'

---

**Lilliana Rose's** short stories and poetry are spreading their wings around the world. She completed her Masters in Creative Writing in 2012 at Adelaide University. *Creating Wings* is her first collection of poetry (2012).

# To My Son

Matthew Gabriel

To My Son Whom I Love Dearly,

It is not your fault that you are ugly, nor is it mine. If you blamed your grandfather on my side of the family tree, you would be closer to the truth. Let it be said that he blamed his own father and his father's father. From my memory and photographs—yet, I wouldn't trust the realism of family portraits from that era—I admit they were not as ugly as your grandfather. You and I also faired a little better, but my father declared, when he addressed the issue, that love should be sought beyond your own farmhouse.

In fairness, it is not what you think. It must be understood that these were different times, and the farmhouse, so to speak, was shared by a number of families—distantly related, that is correct, but nothing unseemly. In my research, members of the local historical society stated that we Gladstones had by reputation through the town been declared to have the face of sin itself. Take note that I was shown a number of sources from their records that confirmed this assertion.

Your grandfather's anger, I believe, was directed towards his mother for not having cycled a little further down the road to seek out a non-Gladstonian dance partner to escort her to the local Mechanics Institute. Although it must be said that he protested my suggestion of both his anger and ugliness, when I finally had the courage to confront him in his final year. Yet, I can attest that my grandmother put up with more than her son's ugly head. She was a beautiful woman of infinite patience, as I too am a good person and I am sure you will be also. Your great-grandmother's only weakness, not to speak ill of the dead, or at least the dead I knew and liked, were those genes and their recessive tendencies. Not one of us got her family's regal forehead, or even her petite and distinctive feet.

In all, I am not sure what the stories my father told me were ever intended to mean, and so now I leave you the first in a series of letters that will make, through the clarity of my exposition, the meaning of your life, I hope, a little clearer. This is a legacy to pass on, should you have the fortune, like me, to have your own children.

It is with respect to this legacy that I accept the truth of my own ugly exterior and reveal to you the measures I have taken to manage this. In past generations, people were more accepting of the idiosyncrasies of nature and taste. Bless, my mother and grandmother. Now, in this era, we stand under the spotlight, no, better still, we stand beneath the steely glare of a 20 metre model's eye on a billboard selling face cream. I admit, it has been described as my obsession—your mother was also very patient—however, through extensive research, I have come to my own conclusions that our ugliness, your inheritance, is both an objective and quantifiable truth.

Yes, I hear your—or is it my father's?—voice protest that we Gladstones have it good. We are intelligent, healthy, able and willing citizens. We need to take pride in giving to others. Although, I find it hard to get my father's scorned and contorted visage out of my mind's eye, as he yelled this advice to me as a child. I had come home from a hard day of reckless and cruel games in the playground, which upon my recollection seemed to revolve around my personal ostracism and debasement. As an only child, I accused my father of not wanting to play with me, just like the other children. It was a vivid reaction I recall, a grown man hiding behind his newspaper to avoid looking at me. It is necessary, at this point, to give some background on your grandfather and inform you that he never subscribed to my theories, and the previously attributed 'blame' only came after sustained pressure on my part, albeit in his last days, to finally admit with temerity and honesty what he had denied throughout my life.

Yet, I stop myself, for it is neither my father's past, nor mine that I wish to dwell upon, nor for which I write this letter, but instead for you to understand your future.

Your mother claims that you are too young for the truth—or as she feels the need to describe it, my callous disregard for your self-esteem, or, and I quote your mother here, with reference to myself, 'the only thing ugly about you is your destructive self-obsession and selfish fascination with your own ugliness *[Pause. Insert accusatory finger point. Lift voice to maximum human volume.]* and it has become awfully ugly'. See I am not afraid of the truth, as I am sure with my guidance, neither will you shy from it. Yet it is here, in this letter, on your first birthday, that I prove to you that my efforts and obsessions have had only one focus, you.

So with no more delay, I hereby officially grant you, my son, Patent #4456A534 for 'The Non-surgical Face Brace for the Betterment of Personal Engagement with Others.' This patent, approved and taken out in your name, Justin Gladstone, across territories worldwide, will, frankly put, make you pigswill rich. A lot richer than the inheritance you would have received. For although you may have heard I am a highly skilled industrial chemist, I'll admit I have also been a long term job market non-participator, who, as an aside, one of the lawyers at the family court described as a financial wreck and a train ticket away from bankruptcy. She had a good wit. Even I laughed at those descriptions of myself. However, when I received the letter that granted your patent approval, albeit alone, I will admit, I laughed louder and longer.

The details, the plans and the drawings for the *Gladstone Face Brace*—the company name has been registered—are clearly outlined in the attached patent documentation, and it is in realising the full potential of my work that I now offer you the following advice.

Firstly, you must be wary when dealing with others, particularly those wearing suits. Do not under any circumstances sell, or let lapse your patented rights. Many an engine, fuelled by spit and sand, sits on the dusty shelves of oil companies. And what are we left with? Not to be glib, but it seems only to sunbake our way through the winters and wait for flood and fire. So, while we still have a world, this is a lesson: do not, under any circumstances, let the cosmetic barons kill the wider Gladstone vision. My invention and your rights to this invention will radically change, no, reinvent the place in which we live. Let us not only rid the world of ugly's plague, but also its inextricable and toxic inverse.

The use of product #4456A534 must spread, for I am not the only person to feel that the one I hold dearly makes those in their company uncomfortable, even at this, your most innocent of ages. Nor am I the only person to feel other's repulsions reflect my own presence. In fact, it is the beauty industry that has paved the way for the reinvention of the Gladstone name. Their PR people and marketers have an obsessive hatred for people, which thankfully has resulted in intensive campaigns to perpetuate permanent insecurity and create whole populaces burdened by their own inadequacy. This in turn has formed torrents of commerce, in the trillions of dollars mind you, with each cent ready for redeployment to the Gladstone revolution. Therefore, with pride I leave to you this generous bag of gold, secured and assured through your approved patent, and also, in the dawning of this new era—shaped by the *Gladstone Face Brace*—a world in which the conditions for interpersonal human engagement will be changed forever.

Secondly, don't sell the *Face Brace* too cheaply. Price is essential in considering your market. Do not drop below the threshold of trust, like the cheap curry that I used to eat often, and that your mother, in fear of her life, went to great lengths to avoid eating.

Please understand that our courtship was difficult with my near empty pockets, and one of the few places that I could take her was, I will admit, at best a bain-marie slophouse claiming a very tenuous affiliation with the sophisticated cuisine of West Bengal. It seems upon reflection a connection made solely through signage. Yet, at $5.75 for two curries and rice, including a scoop of lassi in a plastic cup, I had no misconceptions, but the overreaction from your mother was directly a result of her believing the impossibly cheap, better still, the untrustworthily cheap prices would in all likelihood cause a sudden case of premature death. The only time she agreed to join me ended up costing her three days in bed. I, on the other hand, was left untouched and ready to dine another day. Never forget that this, my son, is the power of pricing on the human mind.

My suggestion, like housing, like cars, is to have your customers commit to the value of your product. The longer they commit, the deeper their psychological investment. I suggest aiming at a price that takes—repayments calculated on a median wage—a buyer at least five years to make a decent dint in the principal. Once their *Gladstone Face Brace* has been personally fitted and installed, they will not only see the immediate benefits, but the value in your product. They will see a growing reduction in other purchases, from 'retail-therapy' and 'purchasing-pain-relief', to lifestyle and self-enhancement products. I don't mean to get ahead of myself, but with the release of the *Gladstone Face Brace*—and yet to be developed, but trademarked, *Gladstone Body Brace*, another great product that will be able to be installed to any-body's body, even children, made from Gladstone's special formula of silicon, latex and biocompatible non-degradable human-protein derived polymers—we will see the benefits of the neutralising of physical appearance in interpersonal engagement with others. The Gladstonian symmetry and tautness, once given to the people, will show immediate and substantial levelling of the 'beauty quotient differential' across all sample populations—but, and this is important, it will also result in the seizing and eventual stalling of the cogs and wheels of the global economy. Despite what some analysts, namely your eternally pessimistic and inherently green-eyed Uncle Dave, may think.

It may strike you that said conditions and claims would not favour the Gladstones and their emergence as a fledging global corporate player. However, as the world leader in a product that by all predictive indicators will revolutionise the needs of all, I can only see such economic downturn or recession as beneficial. The pre-Gladstonian mindset would see this as a means for annihilation of competitors; a necessary correction if we are to enter the new Gladstonian age. Those with the ability to adapt will find the means for securing the loans needed for the only product, beyond basic necessities, worthy of purchase. Those who cannot adapt will be left to wither on history's grapevine. This is what would have happened to you, my dear son, had I not the willpower and the innovation to rewrite the rules of the world for you.

Don't mistake me for a fool. I have no delusions. I understand the work that needs to be done. Our path, the one we have chosen, will be difficult. I have spent time preparing the ground, tilling the soil, but there are some constraints beyond my control. I am a man of moderate means and although my talents are driven, they are constrained to specific fields. I tried to engage others in our project. The people I approached were unable to envision what was so clear to me and I am sure will be plain to you.

Marketing, I am certain, will be essential and I have tried my best without expert help. You will find secured on my computer mock-ups and altered images of celebrities that I have selected to wear our product. These may disturb you at first. The *Gladstone Face Brace,* when first applied and seen, does disturb a person's expectations. This is only due to conditioning. Note that it is of utmost importance for our product's emergence and foothold in the market to change that conditioning for a critical mass of people.

Alas, I had chosen you to lead our research and development in best practice for altering personal expectations in the engagement of others. I had prepared and manufactured a series of *Gladstone Face Braces* to be worn throughout your physical development. They were to be worn alongside a series of braces designed for myself, and your mother. I had developed a reusable brace for visitors, and although it lacked the higher-end features of a permanent fitting, I believed it would be pivotal in anchoring the *Gladstone Face Brace* in all of your critical psychosocial developmental stages. However, let it be said, it was at this point that your mother—who was truly supportive of my endeavours, not specifically related to this project, more in the general sense—and I, began to see things differently.

I had prepared your braces prior to your conception. Yet, it was the foundation for the idea that, in hindsight, should have been my focus. I needed to be more open about the project that was, at this point, classified for my eyes only. Greater transparency, I am sure, would have changed the situation with your mother, but I felt I could never be too careful. In terms of the success of the project, I believed it would be important for us, your mother and I, to be fully installed in our braces as the idea of you came into the world.

I surprised her, and this I know now, was a mistake. I sat on the edge of the bed with my newly fitted *Gladstone Face Brace.* Over to my left the limp latex-silicone of your mother's brace waited for her. In hindsight, the image of a flaccid side of plastic skin, not unlike a deflated football bladder, was not the best way to communicate my ideas, nor my ambition. 'A creepy obsession,' were the words she used to describe the brace and left just weeks after this incident.

I never had the chance to show her the scale of my vision, and I think now, having read the books I have read, from communication and business experts across the globe, that if I'd treated it more professionally, pitched the idea, shown her the mock-ups, the draft patent, and presented the road-map, such as I have begun for you in this letter, then I would be able to tell you all of this, when you were old enough to understand, in person.

Let it be said that it is my choice to have never met you. As it stands, all I wait for is my simplest of demands to be met: to look at you through the eyeholes of my *Gladstone Face Brace.* I refused to accept access, as granted by the courts before your birth, until this primary demand was met. Take note, that even though I was refused entry into the courts with my brace—I am now vigorously pursuing my rights at this moment to make forcible 'public enhancement masking' removal, as it is coming to be known in certain legal circles, an illegal act—I deinstalled on the premises to make my demands for you.

My father and his father, as I mentioned earlier, tried their best to guide me in the world. They attempted to assist me in understanding how best to live, but only left me more confused, as they lacked the vision, the certainty and the legacy that I have left you. Don't get me wrong, there was a certain quality in my inability to clearly understand, or to fully see these men, for who they may have been, that left me with a heavy heart. However, when you are old enough to read this letter, and the letters that will follow, I ask you to accept the invitation I extend. Come and see your father. Already I feel more comfortable in the presence of others, clad in my *Gladstone Face Brace,* and I hope that upon the installation of your own—according to the attached patent description and installation instructions—we can look at each other, bound together by the symmetry, tautness and ageless qualities of our braces, in which you will be able to see me with precision, clarity and openness.

With expectant hope,
Martin Gladstone.

---

**Matt Gabriel** is currently completing his Masters in Creative Writing at the University of Adelaide. He has been published in *Meanjin* and *Best Australian Stories.*

# Antiques

Bernadette Smith

A four-hour drive north and it never matters what time I leave, the sun still hits through every window of the car. It's late summer and the farms are active with hay bales in every other field, each bale at such-and-such a distance from the next and each facing the same way. In the driveway, the line of gums is thick with spit-fire clumps: little welcome packages.

The house would be impressive if you didn't know what was inside; the large rooms congested with storage boxes. There are no surfaces for the dust to show but you know it's there. Rugs are everywhere: Turkish, a few geometric pastels, one cow skin. The colours, though faded, lend the walls a whiteness they don't actually have after a decades-long assault from tobacco. The blinds are shut but sun gets in through bent slats. My mum, covered by a blanket, reaches out for her staple: a too-hot cup of tea and dry salt-less crackers.

'I can't stay long Mum. I'll have to leave in a few days.'

She makes a discreet throat noise of acknowledgement without looking up from her crossword. I want to turn the lights on to check her colour, not that I can ever determine anything, and she'll just scold me for the light in her eyes even though every bulb in the house is only 40 watts. She seems well but maybe I'm just getting used to it; she is tucked so neatly away out here.

When she goes to bed I commandeer her blanket and begin my letter but I only manage one page tonight and even that is a struggle. The metaphors of violence to be imposed—humiliating and past due—lack my usual grace. I just can't get myself worked up lately; it has been one year after all: one year and thousands of words trying to get it right. I date and fold the page neatly and will add it to the shoe-box when I get home. I wish I lived in the age of the letter writer.

✦

'My mum is sick my mum is sick don't leave me now—'

'What's wrong with her?'

'Err, um, undiagnosed but family-assured Alzheimer's.'

'What, that one where the whole family goes: *Christ, old mum's a bit batty?* Not exactly life-threatening.'

'But she called last night to tell me to look at the moon because it was brilliant and she called the telescope *the seeing-eye thing*.'

Her look lets me know she thinks this line of dialogue is unbecoming. She: who used to force the trips to the country especially in winter, who adored my mother's slightly askew stance on all things status quo, joining in after bottles of wine to dissect the sins of Archbishop Mannix.

'You've been pushing for this,' she tells me. It's a fact apparently. Therese has many facts.

'I've been *paranoid* about this.'

'Either way, you've figured it would happen so you made it so.'

Conversations swarm and stagnate and I can see them but I'm not sure anymore if we actually said the words or if we just knew them. I'm craving details; I want historically accurate settings. I know the season of the morning Therese left—summer of course—but not the day, and I have hours of unplaced dialogue so maybe it all happened that final morning, as the man from the beach waited outside for her in an expensive black car. And I can't remember the last day I picked her up from the shop even though I remember a hundred times before: how if I was early or she was late I would watch her surrounded by the metal and rust and if she was still with a customer I watched too, because she would smile so big when she was with one of them. When she hoisted up the set of armour—full-sized and fully armed—it was effortless, and she would take it inside from the street and kiss it on the cheek and say, *Goodnight baby.*

This is a setting: we are in a coffee shop. We are to buy a bookcase. She knows exactly which one she wants, the wood is practically meat it's so alive. I suspect it will loom too large in her small lounge. Her hair is mostly contained by a scarf—'deliberately messy'—leaving her face open and pure. She is talking about him, the man who waited, and I don't know why she is talking about him and looking at her coffee. 'Therese, you know in many circles it is considered impolite to talk about past lovers.'

'Oh,' she says, 'I thought it was *de rigueur.*' God-awful feigned primness out of a perfect face.

There was a day on a beach when we first met and I got her alone by dragging her by one leg out of the waves, making her cough with laughter. We left him there, a speck with all the other swimmers, and she listed things he said and did so we could laugh more. And I can't remember what she was saying about him this time but we didn't end up getting the bookcase even though we'd been planning it all week.

Before she was assimilated by this southern city, she was brown. We—me and the city—made her white though, dragging her out of the water and then off the beach altogether, and we were wonderfully symmetrical. He once called her reptilian as a reference to her old skin but it is clear now he meant it as a warning to her silence in flight. If it wasn't for her length and muscles she would appear fragile. If caught still in a photo, sitting all curled up and around herself she could even look demure but in movement, outstretched to her six feet, there was a sense of reckoning which was once a good thing.

✦

We are driving to buy a sword for me. A customer of hers is selling and Therese says if I am going to buy a sword it has to be this one, a 23-inch single-edged Qing Dynasty beheading sword. On the drive there she taps the steering wheel constantly.

'So you've got the cash?' she asks.

'Of course. You've seen the sword?'

She turns to me with a smirk that grows big and kind and teethy: seraphic.

'It's beautiful.'

Therese did all the talking. They were familiar with each other. Papers were exchanged and they huddled over the table together with the annual bible for people interested in such matters, slides held up to lights but not offered to me, I just produced a cheque upon request and we left with a velvet-laden case. Therese's fingers traced the carvings on the pommel and explained symbols and forging techniques but I didn't care, I just liked it.

She mounted it on the wall for me and when we told Mum about it, she called it ghoulish. Therese was always trying to do things to Mum's house and they would wander around, Therese flailing her arms about and talking about *Space with a capital S* and Mum would look back at me and roll her eyes with mock exasperation but would always make sure she kept up with her, kneeling down when instructed to see invisible things from the right angle.

✦

Mum doesn't feel up for a walk so I go out alone with the dog. The sky is too big out here. I sit at the creek amongst the gold wattle which has gone crazy in this area—you can see the smell. I consider lying prostrate on the stiff grass but the dog is getting restless and wants to walk on. It used to be a good break coming up but now it is tiring, although I've stopped correcting Mum about everything or defending the doctors who are apparently Hysterics. We play backgammon and drink tea and smoke cigarettes and it stays light outside for ages. Mum watches the news and I curl up on the couch and begin a letter. After a bit she asks what it is I'm writing all this time and I can tell by her voice, its determined flatness, that she's been wanting to ask me for ages. Maybe I make faces when I'm writing.

I look at Mum, her bruise of yellow-purple skin, and marvel at how thin her wrists are as she stirs her tea.

'I'm writing an historically accurate record.'

'Ah ha!' She points at me with the teaspoon. 'So you won!'

When she sees that I don't get it, she explains.

'It's history right? And history is always written by the winner. Not that it matters what you write of course, or how many readers you get. It's how good you feel about the winning that counts.'

I crack up. This woman.

'So what do you call what the loser writes?'

She scrunches her nose, wipes it with the back of her hand in serious contemplation.

'Well, that's just propaganda.'

And with the subtleties of subjectivity once again eluding my black-and-white mother, I refocus on the letters that swarm when I get going, a comprehensive list of wrongs and ugliness starting from the day in the ocean. I re-read my last line but the momentum has passed so I sign-off and fold and date the pages and prepare for bed.

In the morning she is asleep in front of the television so

I leave quietly. Her colour seems improved, a nicer shade of yellow. I leave earlier than planned because I was seeing me there in a hundred years, smoking too much and losing colour hand-in-hand with the rugs.

✦

Back home it is hot. Everything reflects the sun and there is a sprawl on the sidewalk. *Oh look at that blouse. What a large mango.* A man offers the mango to his spouse to sniff and squeeze and they are all so pallid in the sun. If I saw Therese here among the cattle we might stiffly embrace with *you look goods* and *it's been so longs,* as though greeting the other after an absence rumoured to be prison time of an unspecified crime. But this scene is wrong because we know what the crime was. That line of men.

I start going out again, sitting with my face pressed against the window in taxis that fling me around the city to every place and yet I never see her. People I know refuse to listen anymore and strangers at closing time are shouting about their own injustices. This is not sustainable. I decide something, the same thing I decide every night before it's erased by the dawn: I must cower until spring, yes, yes! a vernal resurrection into middle-age with accoutrements of good health and sobriety and a mortgage. Oh, oh and monogamy, orgasm-free and dry, and a bright white room-sized fridge with frozen goods, with Tupperware bursting.

---

**Bernadette Smith** studied creative writing at The University of Adelaide. She has published some short-stories and is working on her first novel.

# Olive/Oliver

## Jessica Clements

### 5.

Oliver holds the packet of gum high in the air, the plastic wrapper shiny with his drool, and then throws it on the ground and laughs. He knows his mother will have to bend down and pick it up, and that is part of the game.

'Cheeky boy,' says the checkout attendant whose white name tag reads 'Ruby'. She pushes the first of Anna's groceries over the scanner. 'What's his name?'

Anna bends down to collect the packet of gum, placing it back into her son's chubby hands. She pushes the trolley forward. 'Oliver,' she says.

'Oh!' Ruby says, getting a proper look at the baby. 'Well… he has beautiful eyes.'

'Thank you,' Anna says. She is getting more used to that pause; the hesitation when people first set eyes on her son. His features are becoming more prominent now, though he is still young enough for people to take a second look at his slightly larger than average forehead and wide-set eyes that are piercing and blue like his father's.

Oliver proudly waves the green packet in front of his mother, shrieking with joy.

Ruby hands Anna the first of the filled re-useable bags.

'He certainly seems like a very happy little boy,' Ruby says.

'Yes,' Anna agrees, 'he is happy.'

**4.**

Anna reaches over the mountain that is her belly, pressing against the blunt corner of an elbow.

'I think we should talk about this,' Reid says. He stands in front of the couch, two fists clenched at his hips.

'There's nothing to talk about,' she says. She takes a long breath in, counting to four, and holds it before she lets go. The doctor said it was important for her to stay as calm and unstressed as possible, especially in the third trimester. But it isn't easy with Reid standing in front of her, refusing to leave. 'I told you,' she says calmly, 'you didn't have to be a part of this. We're not married.' She closes her eyes for a moment, keeps counting breath. 'I can do this on my own.' No, she thinks, I *want* to do this on my own.

'You're just saying that because of what I said about that kid at the park,' Reid says.

Anna pictures the look on his face as they saw the mother and child pass them, the boy shrieking and clawing at his mother like he was half possessed. *And that kid's normal,* Reid said.

'Yeah,' she says, opening her eyes, 'that's exactly why I'm saying this.'

**3.**

Anna is instructed to look away as the needle is inserted.

'We're going to give you a local first,' the doctor tells her, 'but you might feel some discomfort as we reach the placenta.'

She pictures Reid in the waiting room, flipping through

the only blokey magazine in the pile, something with cars or girls in bikinis on the cover. She imagines his hands clamming up from the hospital smells and new mothers wheeling past with their newborns, and begins to feel nauseous.

'Deep breaths now,' the nurse says, picking up Anna's hand.

She turns her head and tries to focus on the hand that is clutching hers. The nurse is young with long thin fingers and nails painted olive, a deep shade of green that reminds Anna of her grandmother's kitchen and the wafting smells of baking and warmth. Olive, she thinks to herself. Oliver.

## 2.

'One in seventy. That can't be that high, can it?' Reid says.

'One in three hundred is considered high-risk, so yeah, one in seventy is high.'

'But it's not *that* high,' he says.

'I guess not, I don't know.' Anna admits. She is still trying to process the information the doctor gave them, but the words *high risk* and *Down's syndrome* are playing on a loop inside her mind. It had only been a few weeks since her first eight-week scan. The picture was still taped to the fridge, the foetus nothing but a non-descript blob amongst the dark sea of her uterus. She had just been getting used to the idea of being pregnant when she went in for the second scan. Now everything seems unreal to her again, as though she's still watching it all through the black and grey screen in the radiography room.

'Well, anyway,' Reid says, 'at least they can catch it early so we have options.'

'I'm keeping it no matter what,' Anna says, surprising herself.

'What? Come on, you can't say that. What kind of life would it have?'

'You mean what kind of life would you have?' she snaps. She turns away and wills herself not to cry.

Reid raises his arms in defeat. 'Well, aren't you thinking about that?'

'Yes,' she admits. 'But it doesn't change anything. Not now.'

'How can you say that?'

She puts her hands over her mound, no bigger than a belly full of food.

'Anyway,' Reid says. 'There's no point arguing about it now. Not when we don't know for sure.'

**1.**

Anna hands Reid the white strip, the two blue lines facing up, and watches his face change as he understands their meaning.

'What do you think?' she asks him. She tries to keep her voice even, without hope or anticipation. She can't expect him to be happy about this. They haven't been dating that long.

'A baby?' he says finally.

'Yes.'

He looks up at her, a slow smile creeping over his face. 'She would be beautiful, wouldn't she?' he says.

'It could be a boy,' she tells him, trying to hide her relief.

'No,' Reid says, shaking his head. 'It will be a girl.'

'How do you know?'

'I just do,' he says. 'A little ballerina.'

'No way. A scientist.'

'A rock star then,' he says, as if it's some kind of

compromise between the two.

Anna shakes her head and smiles. 'Maybe a rock star.'

Reid puts his hands around her waist and brings her in, kissing her on the forehead. 'As long as she's happy.'

'Definitely,' Anna says. 'As long as he's happy.'

---

**Jessica Clements** holds an MA in Creative Writing from the University of Adelaide. Her work has appeared in various literary magazines and was shortlisted in the University of Adelaide's first annual Hearsay Literary Competition.

# Roses for Lungs

Annabel Evitts

> *Love is a shadow.*
> *How you lie and cry after it.*
> *Listen: these are its hooves: it has gone off, like a horse.*
>
> Sylvia Plath, *Elm*

*Remember the feeling of stillness. Remember the comfort that the night used to give you—the in-between sky that flamed and died, flamed and died over and over.*
*Remember the sounds that made your blood sing.*
*Remember the sea and the rhythm and the cycles of the earth that turn infinitely, despite your joy or your pain or your sorrow.*
*Remember that red thread of want that descended from your belly.*
*Remember what it is to be loved.*

These are the things that Violet thought of all through the emptiness. And when she could think of nothing at all, her body would seek out extremes: heat that would make her skin numb, drink that thickened her tongue and her dreams. She would starve herself of food until she felt a black kind of hollow open up in her gut like the spreading of wings and when the weakness began to feel like a dream, she felt more powerful than ever. She devoured the mouths of others, strangers that left marks upon her skin, bruises like flowers, salt on her tongue. She carried their scent. But when the heat settles, what is left? The black and white of life—the negative that everything else is hung upon—breath, the beat of the heart, rhythms. Hunger fades away. Art is the thing that makes her feel most alive.

✦

She first went to a gallery as a child with her sister and mother and they surveyed every work up close and from a distance, each in black boots, arms linked together. She loved the silence of the wide-open rooms and the secrets that curled up there beyond the frames. It didn't always feel like silence, for the colours made so much noise. She felt the paint in the way that some people can feel words: red made her heart quicken, blues slowed her blood down, brown felt cold and thick as mud—it became a kind of language that her body spoke. A little slice of that world would imprint upon her, like a tattoo under her skin, like a haunting, and the outside world would bend out of shape or be transformed almost completely. Art was not static: it moved and moved things within her. This is why she became a painter, why she buried herself in the history of art. It made her remember and forget all at once. The emptiness still comes sometimes, crawls on all fours towards her and nestles in her chest. It comes on wet streets, by the glow of café lights; it comes in offices, bookstores, galleries and restaurants, on highways and in corridors, in bedrooms and in theatres. It trails her like vapour. *Remember the sounds that make your blood sing.*

✦

As Violet walked home, she drew a breath down deep into her lungs and the cold sat there and turned solid. There was the scent of rain, but no water. The trees quaked in the wind as it built. She thought of one of his paintings: a woman lying naked on an open road, a storm, and in her chest, wild roses, vines curling around her ribs. She held a whole other world inside her.

This was so true of Leonard. It was as if he had taken his body and transposed it somehow, across gender, across space and time, into that painting. He had always been a magnetic man, charismatic, intelligent and yet there was something polarised in him, something hard to define, like he was keeping a secret, or keeping some fundamental part of himself hidden away, that might only be glimpsed in a fleeting, unguarded moment. Sometimes, the change in him was so subtle that you might have been convinced it was a trick of the light; other times the wildness that rose up and out of him was so exquisite that you couldn't help but be drawn in with him: when he danced, when he drank, made love. When he was high he was so distant he seemed almost out of reach. But you knew he had settled deep down there, in that beauty, in that openness, that wildness that so often lay sleeping. Most of the time, these feelings of abandon remained tucked away, like small clandestine frenzies. And although he was stoic, there was something else beyond it all. He seemed to Violet to be vulnerable as a child.

She continued to walk further through the city towards the apartment block. She ambled through the night, through the mild green scent of the river that moved alongside the buildings and parks and was grateful for the stillness, for the people passing by whose eyes she met in the darkness—it felt like a comfort somehow, a connectedness.

As she thought of Leonard then, it occurred to her that it may as well have been *him* laid out on that road with his insides open to the air. Her mind carried her there, so that she was looking down upon him. The figure that she saw then was unmistakably Leonard and yet not. For this figure was a sublime blend of both woman and man, one that seemed to convulse eerily somewhere between the two.

It was Leonard's lips, though, that mouthed silently to the sky, something inaudible, something desperate and in his face he was overcome. The roses grew in him and all around him, sprouting up from the dust. There in her mind, Leonard was at the complete mercy of the world. (How can you breathe with roses for lungs?)

As she returned home, sweat curled around her upper lip and the flesh of her left thigh began to tremble. She braced herself at the fence and felt herself to be falling, though she was perfectly still.

✦

Violet first saw Leonard in 1975. It was the year that the Vietnam War ended and the summer was heavy and alive, the heat unravelling a new sensuality in her body. She had travelled to New York on exchange as an art student, twenty-seven years old and poor as dirt, but curious, willing to throw away any small hesitation for the sake of the experience. She thought of herself then as a soft and pliable thing, drawing in everything around her and making it a part of herself, so that when all of these pieces fused together she held a mirror inside of her, crowded with light. The freedom of that time was exhilarating; she moved softly, fluid, filled with a kind of restless hunger so that some part of her was always moving, her fingers, her lips, her feet as she was sitting.

She would sometimes go to the gallery after her classes, in the evenings when the heat had simmered down and the light reached out into the rooms in such a way that the art-work seemed to be on fire. It was there, in the gallery, that she found him.

*What is she thinking?*

His voice came from somewhere behind her. Violet didn't take her eyes off the painting in front of her, though she sensed that he was close; there was a smell of something like vetiver and the faint scent of sweat. The room was suddenly overwhelmingly small. She tried to imagine what she must have looked like to him then: this strange, wired girl, thin as glass, hair as red as heat.

*I don't know—I don't even know who she is.*

She took a step backwards so that they were standing alongside one another.

*Empathy is more than that,* he said.

Like this, Leonard first appeared to her as a dark shape in her periphery, a scent. It took a long time for her to look at him, though she couldn't say why—maybe she had wanted to guard the intrigue of that moment. She looked at him slowly, as if she might be taking in a piece of art, and so he was revealed to her in parts: his muscular fingers, the leanness of his frame and the dark of his hair.

The painting on the wall before them was the largest on display. It depicted a woman kneeling half in darkness and half in light, so that part of her face was obscured. At first it appeared that she was hairless, if it weren't for the thin shock of black across her forehead that escaped into the brightness. Her lower half was draped in green fabric and her knees were open slightly. Violet saw a distinct track of blood that flowed down from the inside of her thigh and stopped just above her knee, another trail diverged and spilled out across the canvas. The tips of her fingers were also stained. She noticed a smear of blood, which muddied the woman's right breast, pale as a dove. The contrast of the scarlet against the white dizzied her, but she couldn't look away.

The image recalled a time as a little girl, walking home from school in the winter. A group of boys had started trailing behind her, jeering, calling out names that she no longer remembered. She drove the sounds behind her and pushed uphill through the cold, making tiny clouds with her breath. Then one of the boys, a big blonde kid called Peter, had caught her and shoved her into the footpath.

She lay completely still—like some discarded doll—until she was sure that the boys had left her, then spread her fingers out in snow, the curves of her cuticles like tiny half-moons. She noticed the way in which silence and snow, whiteness and blankness, seemed always to go together. Lifting her head, Violet felt a salt warmth bloom out from her lip and it was then that she saw the blood, a string of perfectly round, red beads fallen into the white. The beauty of that moment unnerved her and the memory of it coiled under her skin.

*She wants to be put back together again.*

Violet turned to Leonard in the gallery that day and the words hatched out of her like a secret. She saw the grace in him then, the youth.

Countless years later, she sees the mortality. Death shrinks away, waiting; it becomes a kind of blind spot with which he might collide at any moment. It is a scar on the skin, a thing of violence, falling apart and all the while knowing you are alive. She watches the colours fade in him and around him, everything bleached as white as snow.

✦

Now, the night is full of dreams, confusion, full of silence and desire. This night, Violet falls into bed beside Iris and doesn't sleep.

This is a dream in words.

This is what white feels like:

*With my fingers I close my eyes and she goes off. And the tide pulls and releases, careless and foaming. She caught you there on a wave of tears. And you sit on the beach and the sand cakes the curve of your feet and the beat of your heart turns a deeper shade of red because you feel at last you are free.*

(There are all these moments that come together). *The flowers are falling apart and my eyes never close, never turn you away. Iris. She caught you on a wave of tears. She caught you on a blue-sky day, she caught you in a stillness. And there were no breaths left. Was it you sweet thing, who wiped the blood from my body? Who sucked my bones clean of pain? There was backwards movement. There was the heaviness of clouds and no way out. Stay awake* (Iris said) *Sing to me, of when your body found its own way, when your blood buzzed, when you stopped giving a fuck.*

*It was like this: there were scratches on the record, there was a catch in your throat, there was the breaking apart and the falling together, the rushing, the diving, the green flow of water, the taste of blood from your bitten lip—the mirror, the smoke, the sex, the wine, the sadness. Time enough with you, and I'll forget my name. Swallow it down, she said. Forget yourself.*

*Begin again.*

---

**Annabel Evitts** completed an Honours degree in 2011, during which time she wrote a novella, *Taste of the Moon.* 'Roses for Lungs' is an excerpt of her PhD thesis, a novel entitled *Sing to Me.* Annabel is inspired by art of all forms and is drawn to that slippery space between poetry and prose, to finding musicality and sensuality within language.

# Pissing Blood for Lucy Liu

Rachael Mead

Ambulance paramedics are like card sharks. Get them together and suddenly you have a fierce competition on your hands, each one throwing down a story full of weirdness and black humour, trying to top the last tale with a gem from their own experience. The table will rock with laughter, chairs will gradually settle onto all four legs and then the next face will lean in. 'Did I tell you about the woman who almost amputated her finger with her cordless phone?' Gradually the stories will build, each more unbelievable than the last until someone throws down their trump card, the story that they've held back, waiting for this very scenario to unleash it. These stories, these jewels of hilarious or macabre misfortune are the hard currency of ambo culture and it's one of my stories, that I slapped down on the table with a competitive glint in my eye, that I want to share with you.

It's one of the charms of this job that you can never sense when life is about to swing so wide of normal that if it hadn't happened to you, you would think the person telling this story a liar of outback proportions. Fact is stranger than fiction. It's only a cliché because it's true.

✦

We were on nightshift in the northeastern suburbs, driving

back to station after a crib stop at Subway. It had been a slow, wet night and we were looking forward to getting into the warm station, cranking back the Jason recliners and maybe even getting a few hours sleep. Our plans for a quiet one were shelved when pulling up to a red light I noticed a woman in the car beside us frantically gesturing for me to wind down the window.

'Someone wants your number, Simon.' My partner grunted a chuckle as I hit the button to lower the glass.

'I think my friend has tried to kill herself. She called me and I jumped in the car but now I can't get her to answer the phone. She lives just around the corner. Can you come?'

Now this isn't standard procedure. Normally jobs are dealt to us from our communications centre but we're also expected to be flexible if the situation seems urgent. Simon pulled in behind to follow her while I got on the radio to tell comms that we'd picked up a job and we'd keep them informed.

✦

After winding through a couple of side streets off the main road, the woman pulled up at one of those newish houses that look like they could be constructed from Lego. It was separated from the street by a postage stamp lawn that screamed rental property. The house was completely dark.

The woman ran to the front door while we called in the address and gathered our kits. The door must have been unlocked as she was nowhere to be seen as we approached. By the time we flicked on torches and entered the dim doorway, the woman was heading straight towards us up the dark hallway at a run.

'Quick—she's in the bathroom—she's slit her wrists.'

As it was my turn to be the attending officer, I took the

lead and cautiously made my way deeper into the house, heading for the only light, which was coming from a door midway down the central hallway.

It was a bathroom and splayed out unconscious across the tiles was a tiny woman, who looked the spitting image of Lucy Liu. To add another layer of weirdness, despite it being winter and lying prone on cold tiles, she was clad only in a white bikini and there was an empty bottle of red lying near her out-flung hand.

Not wanting Simon to catch me gawping, I put down the kit and assessed the situation. She'd had a half-arsed attempt at slashing her wrists, the cuts were superficial but plentiful and there was blood smeared the length of her arms and on the floor. She either didn't mean business or was too drunk to do the job properly. At this point I noticed that she didn't smell particularly drunk. Normally with patients who've drunk themselves into a stupor their fumy breath hangs in the air like petrol. Even being so tiny, it seemed strange that she'd be unconscious from a mere bottle of red. As she was in no danger from bleeding out, I started my spiel, chatting to her in my non-threatening, talking to children, animals and unconscious people voice. Simultaneously, I was starting my observations, the first being properly ascertaining her level of consciousness.

There are a couple of ways to work out if someone is truly out to the world or if they are faking it. One is to rub your knuckles really hard against the sternum. Have a go on someone. They won't like it. The other is to press a pen really hard into the bed of the cuticle. You won't be popular testing that one either. Both the sternum rub and nail-bed press should make you flinch if you are conscious, even if you are lying there, determined, for whatever bizarre reason, to play possum. It's a mark of extreme willpower to supress that 'what the fuck are you doing to me?' wince. Now, you are probably expecting that because she was lying there looking like a scene out of a Hollywood movie, that I went for her sternum rather than the cuticle. Well fortunately, procedure kicked in and out of pure habit I went for the cuticle. In situations like this where there is limited space and the patient is out to it we are trained to avoid what is called the 'flail zone'. Sternum rubs are damned uncomfortable, so if you try one on someone on the brink of consciousness, chances are they are going to lash out and clout you as you are leaning over them, possibly off balance or, if they are in a white bikini, potentially distracted.

She took it without a wince. So, assuming she was out cold, I got out the saline solution and a large dressing and started to wipe the blood from her arms so that I could see which cuts needed more attention. This wouldn't have been particularly pleasant for her but as far as I was aware, she was unconscious and not really in a state of mind to care. Simon was there, ready and willing to assist, but because of the tiny confines of the bathroom he was relegated to watching from the doorway. This meant that he was the one to see her wait until I turned away to grab some more dressings from the kit, then with feline agility spring onto all fours and crack two perfect roundhouse kicks into my unsuspecting kidneys.

She launched me into Simon, which gave her plenty of time to leap up and shove my gob-smacked partner out of the way with a hand straight to the face and take off down the corridor into the darkened rear of the house. Simon quickly hauled me to my feet, keeping an ear cocked to the rich assortment of obscenities now being screamed from the darkness.

He'd got me up and just outside the bathroom doorway

when the house fell silent but for the sinister sound of a cutlery drawer being wrenched open.

If it wasn't for the light spilling out of the bathroom, faintly illuminating her as she started her sprint down the hallway, carving knife brandished overhead, I'm not sure we would have made it to the front door. Dropping our gear, adrenaline and instinct took over. We bolted.

In theory, I knew that there was a small orange duress button on our radios that automatically calls for urgent police attendance. In practice, I was damned if I could find the bloody thing in the dark while running full pelt for the ambulance with a knife wielding psychopath at my heels. I don't actually remember how but apparently I managed to get the radio off my belt.

'Being chased by a woman with a knife—police attendance required.' Apparently, when you have a radio in your hand, even when in danger of being skewered by a Lucy Liu lookalike, you still speak like you have a radio in your hand. That's conditioning for you.

Simon reached the ambulance first and flung open the back. He stumbled on the step and I knew that if I hesitated the banshee behind us would be cracking open my ribs like a roast chicken. Peeling away I raced down the road, thankfully hearing Simon clunk the ambulance's lock into place behind me. It didn't take many paces for reality to sink in. She looked fit, and I don't mean 'hot' fit. I mean the 'she is easily going to outpace me and not be out of breath when she dismembers me' kind of fit. You could not imagine my relief when I failed to hear the sound of bare feet giving chase. I didn't slow down until a backwards glance revealed her pacing like a caged cat on her front lawn. By the time I slunk back to the ambulance both she and her friend had disappeared inside the house, now eerily silent. Simon slid out of the ambulance and handed me a large Maglite. We were both thinking the same thing. A violent and armed patient was inside the house with both her friend and our kits. This meant that she now had access to all manner of restricted pharmaceuticals, an array of surgical implements and a nice soft body to practice using them on.

We didn't have long to worry about what was going on inside. Apparently, it was time for a wardrobe and weapon change. Lucy Liu re-emerged sporting a pair of jeans over her bikini bottoms and a bare razor blade. She advanced towards us, the pool of streetlight illuminating her like a theatre-spot.

The fact that we were both now armed with ambulance issue Maglites did not go down well with our patient. Simon had a look that I interpreted as being distinctly unhappy with the course of events, particularly the shove in the face and the ungainly bolt for the ambulance. He was an army reservist and built like someone familiar with the inside of a gym. So when Lucy Liu held the razor up to the side of her neck and threatened to slash her throat, Simon found it hard to summon more than a shrug. His disinterest obviously triggered something, for not many seconds passed before Lucy Liu had a light bulb moment and decided her time and resources could be better spent using the razor on one of us.

'I'll fucking slit you.' She lunged at us a couple of times and we backed up, keeping several metres of lawn between us, moving slowly apart so that if she went for one the other could crack her with the torch.

After a couple of half-hearted lunges, she again rethought her strategy and made a run for the house. We heard the sound of crockery and furniture coming apart and used the time to repeatedly check the street for the appearance of the police. The first headlights turned out to be a beaten up old Datsun that not even an undercover cop trying to infiltrate a meth lab would be seen dead in. It pulled up behind the ambulance and a wiry young guy unbent himself from behind the wheel.

'What's going on? Diana called me to say Trudie was in trouble—is she alright?'

'Who are you?' The obvious question.

'Trudie's ex.' He'd just taken in the sounds of destruction from inside and started to edge back to the car. 'Has she been drinking?' His face took on a hunted look and he started fishing in his pocket for his keys.

'Hang on mate—you could help us with a bit of background here. Does she have a medical history?'

'Look if she's been drinking, I'm out of here. Diana didn't say she's been drinking. She's laid me out enough times; I'm not up for it anymore. We're over.'

'What do you mean, laid you out? Does she get like this often? Does she have a record?'

'A record? She's a fucking Australian Champion!'

'Australian champion? At what?' (Swimsuit modelling? Domestic demolition?)

'Kickboxing.'

My lower back throbbed in recognition. He took our stunned silence as an opportunity, slid around the car, slammed the door and took off without a backward glance.

As his car left the kerb with an unhealthy belch of exhaust, Lucy Liu the Kickboxing Champion, ran outside and screamed a bit more abuse. This time it was directed at her retreating ex and her vocabulary improved as she was clearly covering well-rehearsed territory.

At this point we could see a couple of cars parked several blocks down the road. To our relief, numerous police appeared to be suiting up, strapping on ballistics vests. Now,

I realise in siege situations that police, unlike on TV, don't park right out the front, but this seemed to be an extreme distance to leave as a buffer. Especially when they had to jog the intervening distance in those vests of Kevlar and ceramic plate, which weigh a tonne. We watched them approach, stop to catch their breath half way, and then close the remaining distance.

They took up position at the side fences while the sergeant approached us for a breakdown of the situation. I filled him in on what had transpired, ending with the caveat, 'Be careful—she kicks like a mule.'

'Don't worry, son. We know what we're doing. Just leave it to us.' With that we were dismissed with a flip of his hand.

At that point, you would've had to drag us away. Lucy had spotted the cops and turned her tongue on to them. Disappointingly, she was now armed with some broken crockery rather than the razor but still, she managed to put up some fierce resistance.

A handful of cops swarmed in, each one grabbing a limb, throwing her to the ground and pinning her there. The sergeant, who was holding one of her legs, turned to us, I'm sure to let loose some smugness along the lines of 'And that's how it's done' when Lucy Liu, paying stunning homage to Charlie's Angels, wrested her leg free of his grip and delivered a textbook front kick to his chest, dead-centre.

In my mind's eye I can still see it; the elegance, the justice of it as, in Hollywood slow motion, this hefty middle-aged cop arched backward to land stolidly on his arse.

✦

It wasn't until later that night that I thought about fear. Why was this particular job so different, not just in the bizarre details, but in my complete failure to register the real extent of the danger or even experience fear as the situation unrolled?

As we headed back to the station, Simon and I debriefed, laughing over the elements that made the night so unbelievable. Back in the warmth of the station's kitchen I put the kettle on for some tea, realising once I was there that I still hadn't eaten that Subway. Now the adrenaline had ebbed, I was tired and starving.

I wolfed down the tea and the foot-long, decided to try to catch a nap and wandered into the toilet. It wasn't until I was looking down at the blood splashing across the white porcelain that I felt my first true pang of fear that night. As would be standard for any ambo, I called Simon to come and have a look. We stood for a moment's silent reflection over the bowl.

'I think *you're* the next job, mate.'

✦

At the Royal Adelaide I was given star treatment in Emergency, with an immediate bed and lots of concerned nurses, who were more than willing to be regaled with the first retelling of the night's eccentricities. It was not long before Leanne, our shift manager, arrived all fluster and apologies.

'I would've insisted you that come straight here but you sounded so calm on the radio—I thought it was all under control.'

How under control can 'We're being chased by a woman with a knife' sound? But for me, hearing Leanne's reaction to that radio call revealed one more peculiarity of the incident; my unusual state of mind. The danger had unfurled so swiftly, so unexpectedly, that I acted on pure instinct. Those kicks to the kidneys shot so much adrenaline into my system that I was insulated from the fear. That burst of adrenaline protected me from both fully grasping the depth of the danger I was in and being paralysed by it. It's when you have time to think that the fear spreads through you like poison, eating away at the fight or flight response and leaving freeze as the default. If I'd pulled up to that house knowing that inside we'd find a patient who'd had her medical records flagged with 'can be violent when intoxicated' the situation might have played out quite differently. If the call had come through regular channels, comms would've been able to elicit enough background on Lucy Liu's past encounters with police that we wouldn't have got anywhere near her without police presence. I probably wouldn't have ended the night in hospital pissing blood. But then again, a beautiful Australian kickboxing champion wearing a white bikini wouldn't have chased me at knifepoint. And I certainly wouldn't be placing this card down on the table in front of you. Trumps.

---

**Rachael Mead** is a South Australian poet and short story writer whose work has been published in literary journals in Australia, the US, Taiwan and Ireland. In 2013, she was shortlisted for the Newcastle Poetry Prize and her poetry collection, *The Sixth Creek*, was published by Picaro Press.

# Wabi-Sabi

Katherine Arguile

*Unfurling cherry*
*Blushes, droops, for want of rain*
*Dying much too soon*

Like Morse code, the sun's rays flashed on and off, on and off the mirrors of water between green paddy rows as their train trundled past. That's rice, her mother said, and Sakurako puzzled at how such slender grass-like shoots could turn into the rapture of a bowlful of steaming white rice.

Sakurako leaned into her mother's body. As the train swayed them in unison, she felt her mother's ribs knock against her head. Gazing up at her profile, she still thought her lovely, even though her cheeks were now hollow, making her look too old, too weary.

They had not brought any rice back with them; all her mother had been able to trade for their bags of *hōji* tea were the same dusty, wrinkled old sweet potatoes, again. There was no more barley. Green vegetables could be found if one knew where to look, but cost three times as much. Supplies of meat and fish were gone long ago. Nobody knew how long this war would last. Sakurako's mother made the decision that whatever she could find to keep her family alive the longest during this endless privation was the best choice.

The stock of tea from their shop was running low. She did not share her fear with the children: What would become of them when this ran out and they, too, were reduced to eating grass, worms, or dumplings made with sawdust, as some of their neighbours had started to do?

On the island where I grew up, her mother would say, we grew our own food and caught fish to eat. We would not starve if we were there. And her eyes would grow unfocused, gazing at inward horizons. Sakurako knew not to ask questions. She knew that her mother, her exceptional beauty exchanged for a handsome dowry, had been sent over a thousand miles away from Okinawa, where she was born, to Tokyo, to marry her father, but that was all.

At home there remained just a thin layer of rice in the kitchen crock, saved for honoured guests. Whenever Sakurako, her brother and sister played the Eating Game, they hauled off its wooden lid and peered in, imagining that the rice was to be prepared for them. They arranged their drawings on the table, of bowls of earthy *misoshiru* with glossy, slimy *nameko* mushrooms, cubes of tofu and sweet green cress, of stewed pork and ginger, of spinach and pounded sesame sauce. Next to these they laid out pictures of dishes piled high with yellow *takuan* pickle and sweet egg omelette. These were the simple, familiar things they craved. They would sit around the table with *chawan* rice bowls filled with gravel from their father's garden—don't you chip your *chawan,* now, warned their mother—and take up their chopsticks. *Itadakima~su!* they would cry, and pretend to tuck into a meal.

The layer of rice in the crock was so sparse they could see the clay bottom through it. They had not eaten rice for a very long time. A month ago an important business associate of their father's had come to visit. The children had stared as their mother scooped a single cupful out of the crock and washed it with care so as not to lose a single grain before steaming it in the smallest pot she had. They clustered around, inhaling the fragrant steam, getting in her way until she had shooed them upstairs where they played out their food game: Fusae, would you like a piece of my salmon? Oh yes please, that would be wonderful. Would you like some more pork cutlet, Kensuke? Why no, I couldn't, I'm quite full, thank you. It was a game, but one accompanied by pain.

Their stomachs were distended, tight like drums and painful to touch. It seemed odd to them that their stomachs should be so empty and yet look so full and round. Their faces were permanently slicked with dirty yellow oozing from their noses. They had grown so desperate with hunger that Kensuke cried out down the stairs - Mother, if he leaves anything, can I have it? And the guest left his rice bowl and his pickles untouched and though this earned Kensuke a brutal beating from his father, it was worth it for his two morsels of rice. They shared it, the five of them, eating a mouthful each, and after they had all taken their turn, one final, tiny portion remained in the bowl. Sakurako reached out a second time with her chopsticks. In the next heartbeat her father whipped a metal skewer from the *hibachi* full of white-hot charcoal and seared her fingers with it. This rice is for Kensuke, her father said, as Sakurako screamed. He is a boy; he should have it, he needs to be strong. Stop your noise, Sakura, or you will be punished again. She cried silent, fat tears, the burned skin on her hand rising into an angry red welt. The girls watched their brother gulp down the rice, tears trembling at the edges of his eyes from the beating and from the pleasure of food in his mouth, and she thought that if she had been given the rice, she would have eaten it grain by grain, making it last, savouring it.

Digesting the mouthful of rice caused Sakurako mild discomfort. After months of eating the same sweet potato gruel, her stomach found the rice too unfamiliar. *Shoyu* or salt had once flavoured the gruel but this, too, had run out. She was so tired of eating the plain gruel that despite the endless gnawing of her hunger she sometimes gagged as she ate.

Even so, Sakurako looked at the *furoshiki* bundle misshapen with gnarled sweet potatoes in her mother's lap as they swayed along in the train, and could not wait for her day's meal when they got home. It was the only way to lessen the grinding ache in her stomach. She wondered whether one day the walls of her stomach and the skin of her back would touch, even though her belly bulged out at the front. At first, her mother had taken in her baggy *monpe* trousers so many times she had given up trying, and they had then been held up with a belt of red cotton rope. Now that her belly was swelling out again, she didn't need the rope any more.

They heard shouting in the next carriage. Her mother's body tensed against hers. Women further along the carriage got up and began wrenching open the windows. The military police! The police are on the train! Hurry! And as they rolled past verdant hills and glittering rice paddies, the women threw their bundles from the windows. Sakurako watched as they rolled down the railway embankment, *furoshiki* popping open, sweet potatoes and cabbages rolling out into muddy ditches and then her mother was standing, pulling at the window, crying: Hurry! Sakurako! Help me! She stood with her bundle at the window and was pushing, pushing, but it would not fit through. The window was too high up for Sakurako to be able to reach up and help. Her mother sat back down, breathing hard, and with shaking hands undid the *furoshiki.* Sakurako passed the potatoes, one by one, to her mother, who hurled them out of the window.

They had barely sat back down again before three policemen burst through the door at the end of the carriage, herding a couple of cowering women before them. One of them thrust out his chest, hand on hips, and bellowed to all in their carriage: Black market trading is an imprisonable offence! It is an act of treason, of disloyalty to our government! Let these women here be an example to you! He shoved hard at the back of the grey-haired woman in front of him. Frail and gaunt, she crumpled like a winter *kimono* slipping off a wooden rack, landing on her knees. Get up! the man shouted. He pushed at her so that each time she tried to rise up, she fell back down. Idiot! Get up! A baby began to wail. Sakurako watched as the women were herded towards the next carriage, where, at the next station, they were taken off the train to nobody knew where.

The train rumbled on; Sakurako watched farmers in the fields hoeing rows of vegetables, tending to rice shoots. She could not understand. The sound of weeping disturbed the air around them here and there. She looked up at her mother, whose dry eyes looked dead ahead. Her mouth was set tight. Only her fingers moved, curling and uncurling around the empty *furoshiki* cloth in her lap, tying and untying its corners.

That night they ate a broth of water boiled with a square of *kombu* seaweed her mother had already used for countless pots of broth; in their bowls floated one dumpling each, made with sawdust and a little flour. Sakurako was so ravenous she nearly swallowed hers whole. Her mother had barely cleared the table before Sakurako had vomited it up in the garden and earned a slap from her father for messing up his treasured flowerbeds. She used his garden trowel to bury it, her knees sinking into the dirt. She wondered if she should collect some of the earthworms burrowing there to eat, like some of their neighbours were doing, but couldn't bring herself to touch them. Her mother was helping Fusae and Kensuke get ready for their bath. Her father was in his study.

With no one else in the garden, she crouched forward, lowering her forehead into the earth, allowing its coolness to spread down to the feverish red spots on her cheeks. The dirt muffled her sobs. She watered the garden with her tears and the soil stuck to her face, mingling with strings of milky-yellow snot. The immaculately pruned shrubs snatched at her hair. The loamy smell of the earth between the smooth stones nourished and soothed her. It smelled good enough to eat. She pushed her lips into it and licked away what clung there. It was gritty between her teeth, but tasted of strength. Her father wouldn't let her mother grow vegetables or potatoes in this earth. She asked her mother why—it was too dangerous to ask him—and her mother had given her a strange, sad smile and said that he wasn't prepared to rip out his azaleas for anyone. They'd been growing there for generations, she said, tended by her father's father and her grandfather's father before that, and it was part of their family heritage, their tradition. The garden was full of poetry, her father had said, full of poetry and beauty. Poetry was eternal, while all living things were ephemeral. If he ripped the beauty out, what would be left?

---

Born in Tokyo of a Japanese mother and English father, **Katherine Arguile** moved from Tokyo to Singapore to Hamburg to Edinburgh to Cambridge before spending eighteen years in London. She is now settled in Adelaide's beachside suburb of Semaphore with her husband and has recently become Australian. When not writing, she works as a barista, strives to run ever-faster PBs and treats her cats like furry children.

# Self Portrait with Angel Olsen

Bryan Whalen

This is what I have done with my life—

Alone, I have moved to the edge of a vast desert to live in a cold apartment with high ceilings, wooden floorboards, a dusty chandelier, and a claw foot tub. There is a large bedroom for my single mattress (with its sharp springs and sleeping-bag blanket) and a large bedroom for my desk (a weathered kitchen table harvested from the street side). On this desk sit stacks of paper, an open laptop, a burning candle that lights little and heats nothing, and a glass ashtray filled with pencil shavings. On the stacks of paper are the hasty and searching sentences that make up the first draft of my first novel. And on the laptop (the laptop open in front of my eyes) is a video that is not pornography. Because yesterday I learned that diddling one's self while watching others engage in loveless sex does not quell the sensation that you are ultimately alone in this world. And you are ultimately alone in this world. Even if you're in a relationship. Even if you're a Siamese twin. We are alone because we will never know what it is like to live behind another's eyes…

At least, these are the thoughts from behind my eyes on Monday, August 27, 2012, at 12:14am. I have not communicated face-to-face with a friend in over four months, have not seen my lover in six, and have not seen my mother in years.

Because I am a binger. (In Melbourne, where I lived pre-cold-lonely-apartment, I binged on friendships and friends, spending hours, days, weeks, and months on couches, at parties, in parks, on road trips and in fits of laughter. I binged on love, as well, sharing every waking moment of the past six years with the woman I would eventually ask to be my wife. Now I binge on solitude, writing and guacamole.)

'Go confidently in the direction of your dreams,' writes Thoreau.

I am living my dream, yes, but what Thoreau forgot to mention is that dreams often get really fucking weird before you wake up.

For example, this morning I was walking back from the market and I said to my lover: 'It's criminal. Three dollars an avocado! And they're not even ripe.' At which point I realised that my lover had followed her respective dream and moved to Europe. We had not spoken in over seventeen days—or is it eighteen?—and I was talking aloud to myself…

Alone, I pushed forward with nowhere to go but here. To this cold apartment. And in this cold apartment I found a note scribbled on the back of a cereal box: *Chapter begins in a home for the disabled. Positive thinking. Leap and the net shall appear. At the end of the chapter a man in a wheelchair rolls himself off a cliff. No net appears, etc.*

'When did I write this?' I asked myself.

'Before you went to the market,' I answered aloud.

The shop attendant had given me a strange look when I stepped into his store, and I had gathered my items (avocados, a brown onion, coriander, tomato and some tortilla chips) and he rung them up with his little laser gun, eyeing me with either disgust or disdain. I had handed him a bill. He handed me some coins.

'You accidentally short-changed me,' I'd said and he looked at the cash register and at me. He opened the register to retrieve my missing bill and I joked. 'If I were a rich man,' I'd said with a straight face. 'I would have you killed.'

But yes, I am writing to myself on a laptop.

Beside this open document is another open document and beneath my wrist, written in pencil on the desk, is a note: *Being alone is fun!*

I should feed myself.

I should make guacamole.

I should write to my lover.

I should be in bed.

But first, I should check Facebook.

Facebook tells me that Matt has a new favourite bagel shop. Hannah has named her chooks Patty and Selma. The love of my life has messaged to tell me that she will message me later. And Jesse has posted a video. *This girl,* reads his comment, *sounds like something between edith piaf and odetta. She writes perfect melodies and as added bonus she's a megababe.*

And so I click.

There is the steady-soft sound of a plucked guitar over white Helvetica size 16 (all caps):

ANGEL OLSEN
LOGAN SQUARE CHICAGO ILLINOIS
JULY 19 2010

The text fades and images appear. An olive-skinned man with blotchy tattoos and a neatly trimmed goatee is staring skyward, as if disturbed by a raindrop. Above him bob the boughs of an elm tree, leaves fluttering and in my ear is the guitar's steadily increasing rhythm.

The olive-skinned man turns to me (to us, to the camera)

and for a moment he is my Uncle in Encino, California, 2002. Dark circles, olive skin. Grandpa Max has died and we are on the way from the funeral to the reception. My Uncle's truck smells of tobacco and marijuana and I am eighteen years old and we have never shared a joint before. 'How do you like college?' he asks, and I say it's great, and he passes the joint and says, 'Sorry I was never around when you were a kid. I didn't want to be a bad influence.' I accept and say it doesn't matter. 'Sorry I was scared of you when I was a kid,' I say, 'but you were terrifying.' He has the eyes of a basset hound, which is to say sad. And I am happy. I am with my Uncle, sharing something.

The olive skinned man looks away from the camera and Angel's voice is in my head. 'Before we draw,' she sings, 'my dear dear friend, I promise you my word. If we should part, my dear dear love, you know you're in my heart,' and that voice could be the voice of my mother, if my mother could sing, and I could be four years old. My head in her soft lap. Her: brushing back the hair from my forehead with warm hands. Me: trying hard to keep my eyes open. On the screen, a shoulder appears (out of focus and covered in a brown sweater) and I miss everyone I have ever known. In focus are the bobbing boughs of that elm tree, leaves fluttering. 'I want to be naked. I don't mean my body. I don't need my body. I am floating away. I am floating away. I am…' And I am on a eucalyptus bed in Southeast Queensland, my lover beside me, staring at the sunlight as it filters through the branches, the earth radiating heat.

On a distant street, a clock tower chimes once, twice, six times. It is six in the morning on Monday, August 27th, 2012, and my cold apartment has filled with light. The morning birds are singing outside the window, and I have watched that video at least three dozen times. But I will soon rise from this computer to eat an avocado grown by some farmer on the other side of the world. I will rise, yes, and stumble toward a single mattress with sharp springs and a sleeping bag blanket. And the birds will chirp. And I will crawl in singing.

---

**Bryan Whalen** has published short stories, essays and poetry in several online and print publications. In 2014 his PhD thesis in creative writing received the Dean's award for academic excellence. Born in Ventura County, California, he currently lives in Amsterdam. To read more of his work visit www.bryan-whalen.com.

# Thank You, Jean Harley

Heather Taylor Johnson

'Truth is, Stompy, she was always tryin to leave. She came too quickly out of the womb. Near tore me to pieces and put me in such a state I didn't know if anything were real or not. Nothin like childbirth. Pain you can't even imagine, but it's a good pain. A right beautiful one. Otherwise we wouldn't keep doin it.' Pearl squinted, trying hard to see into the past. 'I swear when Jean was born she weren't even cryin. And when they brought her over to me that first time, she still hadn't a cried. Just looked up at me with those big blue eyes of hers and stared into my own. I know they say babies don't see nothin but fuzz when they're born but I'm no dummy, Stompy. A mother knows. She was lookin straight into my eyes. She saw me. Just wished I coulda looked into her eyes and seen her when she was dyin.'

The old woman smoothed out the pink and cream woollen blanket with all of its history told in the many holes and stains. The fabric was more scratchy than soft but she liked the feel of it under her hands. It was as much home as the house they'd built in the Ozarks with their own hands, as much as the rich soil surrounding her husband's grave on which the blanket lay. She looked up to the clouds which seemed to spin the earth faster this afternoon. 'Guess there ain't a thing I can do about it now. I just hope she forgives me for not bein there.'

Pearl was sixty-one years old, with a birthday coming up later in the month. She looked and felt ten years older. Worrying about food and clothing can put deep furrows on a mother's face. That, and smoking more than the chimney of the pot belly stove in the small kitchen ever did. And though she wasn't quite sure how she would manage getting up from the blanket she was sitting on, what with her knees so riddled with arthritis, she liked being nearer the earth where her husband rested. They had been picnic lovers when he was alive, so when she visited him now, they picnicked.

'What about that time she went missin? Only seven years old. Wanted to get to the state line. She been studyin that geography in school and thought the line between Missoura and Kentucky was a real line. Like someone took one a them permanent markers and drew one right there next to Hickman.' The clouds had now completely covered the sun and the woman shivered, feeling the chill boring into her shoulders, her fingers and especially her knees. 'I always did blame myself for that. Member how I told her if she could get there she could stand with one foot in Missoura and the other in Kentucky? She liked that. You liked that, too, Stompy. I member you sayin you'd like to go one more. You'd like to stand with one foot in America and the other in Mexico. You member that? Good thing she didn't take up your idea that night.' Pearl looked up, as if the continental border lay in the clouds. 'I also member the moon was big and low that night. We was settin out on the front porch, sharin a can a beer, wonderin if we'd ever get to Mexico one day, or any other country. Didn't even know she done snuck out. Course we didn't ever get to Mexico, did we, Stompy? Even when our girl went and found herself Australia we didn't leave our home. I don't think she was mad at us, though. She knew we were simple folk. But her leavin us like that, livin so far away…didn't think I'd ever forgive her for that. Too painful watchin her get on that plane, but wasn't she a sight? So much spunk, and she was little, too. Short, like you.'

Pearl clasped her hands together, sniffing the mist the clouds contained. It wasn't much different from the morning after Jean had slipped out of the house to find that black line between Missouri and Kentucky, even though it was the end of winter now and it had been late autumn then. A chill was not ideal for a missing little girl in a flannelette nightgown and without slippers. Pearl and Stompy and a neighbourhood of worried souls wore jackets and strong shoes and boots while they joined the police in their search for Jean. Now Pearl wore an old green cardigan and her shoes were white and orthopaedic.

The ageing woman sniffed the air some more, sure she could smell her daughter if she only focused hard enough. 'I thought she was gone then. I never did think anyone had stolen her—I knew better than that, in my heart, and I knew that Curtis fellow was a fine man, even if his skin was as black as the inside of a broom closet. Didn't ever bother me none. Did you, though, but I thought she was gone for sure in a different way. She was old, then. Even at seven she was old. And she was curious, too. A wild seed likes to blow in the wind and that's what that girl was. But we got her back. Dolly Fife's son found her sleepin in that hollow tree, member? She musta been so cold, Stompy. Such a cold ground in those early hours that time a year.' She looked off in the direction of the forested patch of land where her daughter had lost her way long ago, looking for the line. 'But we got her back, didn't we? And she wasn't even scared.' Pearl remembered the love-making that night, too. The shared desperation so strong that it was both physically and emotionally painful, and that the pain was a thing of great beauty.

From a basket with a woven rose near the latch Pearl retrieved a thermos and a plastic container of three peanut butter biscuits. A zip-lock bag with a ham and cheese sandwich cut in two had escaped un-smooshed. She felt relieved, old enough to know that it was sometimes the tiny things that could ruin a day.

'I member when I found out Jean was doin the dirty with that boy from school. I member him, all right. He played the football, but he wasn't very big. Wasn't very good if I member correctly. I reckon she left us then, too. She had that womanly way about her. She was prouder. Wore her shoulders back like this.' The old woman's back cracked twice below her shoulder blades then quickly spasmed above her coccyx. She flinched, though no one would've guessed had anyone seen, such was her way with just getting on. 'I never did tell you. No need to make you angry at your own blood. And you woulda been angry, Stompy. You woulda let that girl have it, through silence anyway. You never did touch her, did you? Just had to look at her the wrong way and she knew she was in trouble. She'd be sorry straight away. Besides, you woulda just said that boy was only sweet talkin so's he could get our Jean pregnant, cause we got pregnant, didn't we? Not everyone is as unlucky as us, Stompy. Or as blessed.'

As the woman poured tea from the thermos into the plastic cup she looked to the trees to find the lone redstart singing *see, see, see,* wondering if it had a partner who might sing back *me, me, me.* Courting is courting, whether it's done by bird or man. Stompy put on airs to win her over. Wore that chequered hat when he was only seventeen, as if he was something too big for their small town. Of course he was tethered to the land by his own blue veins, and that was what had won Pearl over in the end. Each time she thought she saw one of those redstarts in a faraway branch, a flutter in another tree would distract her. It seemed the birds were everywhere and nowhere.

'That boy didn't have to do no sweet talkin to Jean because she didn't need no winnin over. If Jean wanted to be havin relations, it'd be her to do the winnin over. She was a whipper, that one.' There was the bird, its orange underbelly pushing through the limbs of an elm. Pearl rested with ease then, slumping further into her bones. 'I member that boy, too. Long time ago Jean told me he died. He was only young. Felt so bad for our girl when she told me. And for the boy's mama. That's when I forgave her for bein so silly as to risk havin a baby. I member thinkin that I was happy he got to know Jean in that way. Young boy like him didn't need to die no virgin. Glad he got the chance to know what it was to lie down with a girl and have your whole life change. She was a good girl, that Jean. No matter how old she was when she lost her innocence, she was good then and she's good now. Don't know why all the good people have to go and die on me.'

The hot tea felt soothing against the cool breeze at her throat. She knew where the sun had gone, wrapped up in that steady flowing river of white, but still, she looked for it. She closed her eyes, imagining the darkness before her was night time in Australia, and thought about her grandson sleeping. They were separated by distance and age, joined by their love of Jean and an inability to grasp the enormity of life and death, the fact that they could talk on the telephone when it is both today and tomorrow, both yesterday and today.

'Ah, Stompy, how'd it ever get to this?' Pearl began to cry. Outliving a child was the hardest thing a person could be asked to do. Even the redstart had quietened his song out of a curious respect. Animals know death. They know the sound of a mother grieving for her child. 'She didn't have no time to tell that little boy goodbye. She didn't have no time to kiss him goodbye or leave him no note or nothin. Member when she left us for real that first time? Went to Colorado for the summer? She'd left a list for us. She was always makin those lists. I member two things on that list. One was real practical. She said *Put a nail in the wall by the back door so you can hang your keys on them and they'll never go missing again.* Pearl giggled, thinking back to Stompy's old ways. He'd have lost his britches if he hadn't belted them to his waist. In the end, he'd lost his mind, and nothing could've kept it in its place. 'The other was a real sweet one. She said *When Clover has her pups, kiss each one for me.* Member that? Those pups lived under Jean's bed when they was born. When she came home, what was left of them were sleepin on her bed.' The old woman smiled. 'And there was another thing she said, but it wasn't on that list. It was in a note she left for me. She said *Find love with Dad again. Let it in. Hold onto it.* Pearl closed her eyes and breathed in thickly through her nose. Her nostrils flared and her lungs filled and a wave of vertigo came, then left. 'Them were hard times, Stompy. I never thought I was the type to overlook adultery but there I was, and you better thank your dead daughter for that one.' She opened her eyes and looked for a break in the clouds where blue might have a chance. Where sun might have a chance. She wanted to see the geometry of clouds against shafts of light, not the single white plane like an unlined sheet of paper or a blanket of snow in early February or a soft shawl around her cold shoulders. There was no blue, not even a thinning patch where blue might seep in if stretched far enough. But it was okay. If spring wanted to hold onto winter that little bit longer, it was okay. She wasn't going to run to something warmer, something better. This was her home. This was her life, troublesome as it was, but here on this picnic blanket, talking with Stompy and remembering Jean, she knew it to be a beautiful thing. 'Let's both thank her, Stompy.'

---

**Heather Taylor Johnson** is the author of three poetry books and one novel. She is a poetry editor for *Transnational Literature* and has been known to teach Creative Writing at the tertiary level. She began her PhD at the University of Adelaide in the first year it was offered. It took her six years to complete, and she blames her babies.

# The Blood, the Snow, the Raven

Katherine Doube

It is true that while she sat by the window looking out into their snow-covered yard she pricked her finger with her needle. She watched as the blood welled. A perfect bulb of red. She had never been good with blood and now, confronted with only a drop, she felt a lightness rising in her head. She pushed open the windows for some air. Blood smeared on the glass. A drop fell on the snow that had landed softy on the windowsill overnight. Red, white.

It is true that a raven landed at that moment on their closed gate and although her first thought was of death—those graveyard birds—her next was to admire the sheen of the feathers, a black of such depth you could drown. It is true that it was at this moment that she made her wish. A child, lips as red as blood, skin as white as snow, hair as black as the raven's feathers.

However, when her husband arrived home that evening, no love was made. Nine months later no child arrived even though her desire was nine months stronger. A fresh wife's boredom nine months longer. The pile of knitted booties nine months high. The snow melted, the flowers blossomed and faded, the grass dried, the leaves began to fall. Her desire like a tropical weed, worming its tendrils into places it didn't belong. Cakes laced with need, knitting pearled with want.

Sleep disrupted like a burst balloon. Small trinkets collected on the windowsill. A small wooden elephant, a kitten made of china, a soft flopping rabbit. A glass milk bottle with teat.

Now there was a growing bud, she could feel it deep in her womb. Blood separate but shared. A nestling space in her centre. A shell filled with nurture.

Again the snow began to fall. From sleep she woke. A knife in her centre. Blood the colour of lips. A shell emptied.

Her husband arrived home with an antique doll. Lips as red as crimson paint, skin as white as porcelain, hair as black as ebony dye. Such beauty a shock. A perfect doll with weighted blinking eyes. Eyes that were blue. A silent gift. Cradled gently, so softly. Love like a feather landing on moss, a breeze as gentle as an eyelash. The perfect child. The perfect girl.

At the window snow fell. Next to the warmth of the crackling fire, mother and doll watched the flakes float on nothing. A raven, again on the gate. Yellow eyes, vital, pierced her own. She placed a hand on the pane, felt the chill enter her flesh. Blood still smudged on the glass, a brown stain against the white landscape. She licked her finger, smeared the blood off the window and pressed it onto the cold forehead of the doll. As cold as the ice sheeted window.

The doorbell rang. Standing on the doorstep was a crone, black hooded, yellow eyed, nose like a beak. *A hairpin for the child,* she crackled and passed over a tortoiseshell comb, delicate carving and sharp teeth. Raven hair was twisted and pinned. The door closed.

In the corner by the fire the porcelain skinned child giggled. The wooden elephant cantered across the hearth. In a crawling hurry, the child followed. Her fat little legs a flurry of un-coordination, she fell, the comb dropped from her hair and shattered on the bricks. The child lay unmoving, cold as the snow falling outside the window. Blue eyes weighted closed.

Sitting again by the window, doll cradled in her arms, she stared out the window. Her heart was chipped. Pieces flaking off like old paint. Love like a waterfall pounding onto rocks, boulders melting away one grain of sand at a time. The raven hopped across the yard. Footprints marking the smooth virgin snow. An avalanche of snow fell from the roof, she bit her lip in fright. The metallic taste of blood spreading over her tongue. She pressed her lips against the forehead of the doll, a lipstain of blood, lipstick on tissue.

The doorbell rang. The crone offered a tray of ribbons. Emerald green, fire red, lapis blue, slate grey. A single pink ribbon, fine like a spider's web, as pink as skin with hot blood beating behind it. She tied it around the neck of her doll.

By the warmth of the fire the girl played, teasing the kitten with a thread of wool. The kitten pounced and tumbled. Paws soft and claws sharp. It saw a thin pink gossamer thread, pounced and caught it. Rolled around, tangling the thread in its paws. The ribbon unravelled. Falling from the girl's neck. She was still, as cold as the avalanche of snow.

With the doll cradled in her arms, she wove thread into knots of love. She watched desperately over the snow covered yard for the raven. Love tightening the tapestry, squeezing the threads tighter than they ought to be. Watching too eagerly for the raven, she pricked her finger, like the first time, and a drop of blood welled. She pressed the sticky blood onto the child's forehead and breathed relief as the doorbell rang.

*This one's for you.* The crone held out an apple, shining red skin. *You have to make a choice.*

She took a bite of the apple, cream flesh juicy and sweet. She felt a piece lodge in her throat, felt the breath cease in her body, felt her blood grow cold.

Her husband arrived to find his home empty aside from a child laughing by the fireside, playing with a familiar looking doll. The child perfect: skin as white as snow, lips as red as blood, hair as black as the feather of a raven.

✦

And the rest you perhaps know. A new wife, beautiful with sparkling yellow eyes, an enchanted mirror and a nose like a beak.

---

**Katherine Doube** has lived in six cities across five countries but has always and will always call Adelaide home. She was not born there and does not live there, but she did complete her PhD in creative writing at the University of Adelaide.

# Lia and Amos

Lynette Washington

Amos's wife is at the bar. Her short blonde hair with its brown roots, her long tanned limbs and athletic waist are trained on the man in front of her. It is summer and Lia is dressed in her favourite way—exposed skin showing off her hard work at the gym. Everything about Lia's body looks familiar to Amos; it is almost like watching himself.

Lia flirts with the man at the bar. She throws her head back and laughs in her deep, raw way that layers joy with sex. She rests a long-fingered hand on the man's shoulder and lets it linger there while she listens to him speak. She raises her champagne to her lips as he raises his beer to his, and lets her hand slip lower onto his bicep, gripping it a little more tightly now, no longer resting. Lia has perfected an almost clinical flirtation process, but it is her intuition that really makes her good at it.

Amos turns his attention to the man now. His body language is just as important as Lia's. In fact, everything rests on his reaction. The man is leaning against the bar and his hips are pointing in Lia's direction. This is one of the signs Lia has told Amos to look out for; 'If he's pointing his groin towards me, he's interested—don't bother looking at his face. It's different for men and women—for women, look at their face, for men, look at where their dick is pointing.'

So this is good, the man is responding to Lia's flirtation. He smiles when she smiles, laughs when she laughs, drinks when she drinks. This is another sign that Lia has taught him to look for; 'If he's copying my actions, he's interested, if he's looking over my shoulder he's wondering if he can get someone better.'

The man is touching Lia's back. His hand rests gently on the small of her spine, a finger casually inching through the belt loop at the top of her short denim skirt. This is good; 'If his touch goes a little bit further than mine, it's a good sign. If I touch his arm, he touches my back. If I touch his chest, he touches my arse.' Lia's mantras are a checklist in Amos's mind.

Tonight is going to plan, but the next step is crucial. Amos waits.

They finish their drinks and place the empty glasses on the bar. Amos watches the man closely and knows he is asking Lia if she'd like another drink. This is the moment. Amos knows what his wife is about to say, and it has to be just right. Some men bolt at this point, although Lia is usually pretty good at picking.

And there it is—Lia leans in to whisper in his ear so that her words can't be overheard. She puts her hand on his arm to steady him and keep him close. Her perfume is drifting up from between her breasts. She is speaking slowly, with confidence and just a touch of vulnerability, although she possesses little of this particular quality herself, just the ability to portray it when required. She is measuring her words. Certain words require gentleness, others require force. Others require sexiness—sexiness is Lia's trump card.

There are a couple of ways this could play out. Sometimes, but not often, the man pulls away as though he's been slapped in the face, looks wild enough to punch Lia and then storms away breathing words like 'disgusting', 'pervert' and 'slag'. More often than that, though, and because Lia has a knack for picking them, the man looks over to where Lia is pointing, towards Amos, and checks him out. At this point, Amos's role is simple: raise his glass in their direction, give a small smile and hold the man's gaze. The message is clear, 'I'm in. Are you?' Then it is all up to the man.

As predicted, the man follows Lia's gaze and looks at Amos. He looks for a long time. Amos holds his gaze, just as Lia has taught him to. He is starting to feel anxious.

Amos sees a faint smile appear on the man's face and he feels his excitement build. This one looks just right, for them both. He signals for Amos to come to the bar and join them.

✦

Amos watches as his wife pulls the thin cotton sheet away from the small sweating child asleep in bed. After a night like the one they've had, he is always astonished that she can switch back to motherhood so easily. Lia turns and leaves the room where their son and daughter sleep peacefully, and goes to pay the babysitter. It is 3am: an expensive night out, even considering the drinks that the man, who Amos now knows as Steven, bought for them.

Amos follows Lia to the kitchen and watches as she makes a cup of tea for each of them.

'It was a good night, don't you think?' she says over the boiling kettle.

'You chose well, you always do.'

Lia smiles, 'I've had some practice now. I know the ones who will get it, and the ones who won't. I can tell just by watching them for a while.'

'But still, it's brave, what you do.'

'You too.'

Lia pours the drinks and puts the cups on the table in front of Amos, then sits on his lap, ignoring the way the arms of his chair gouge her legs. Beneath her, Amos knows she can feel his spindly and wasted legs, but he cannot feel her weight at all.

'We can stop this anytime you want, you know,' Lia says.

'You say that every time. But you know I like it too,' says Amos.

'Yes, but...'

'I know, I'll tell you if it ever changes for me. And you will tell me too.'

Lia leans over and kisses her husband. 'Of course. Shall we go to bed?'

'Sure,' Amos says.

Lia leaves their drinks on the table and wheels her husband into their bedroom. She helps him into his pyjamas and into bed. Because she knows he's tired, she arranges his legs so they can spoon and puts her arm around him, resting it in the valley where his ribs give way to his waist. There she can feel his chest rising and falling more and more slowly as he falls asleep in her arms.

---

**Lynette Washington** spent much of her childhood roaming around Australia in a caravan. Now, she is constantly torn between competing desires for footloose travel and suburban security. Her short stories and flash fiction have been published and awarded and she is currently working towards her PhD in Creative Writing at the University of Adelaide, where she also teaches. 'Lia and Amos' is one story of many in her as yet unnamed short story collection. Twitter: @LynneTashi Facebook: Lynette Washington—Author

# All You Need Is Love

## Anna Solding

The day he got out, the sky was a flimsy, grey film, as if the city had been wrapped up in used sandwich paper. A gust of wind grabbed his jacket and shook it. Sammi had almost forgotten about the wind, the loyal Malmö companion who would always be in your face, no matter where you were heading. One thing that he hadn't exactly missed during his time inside. Two years is an eternity, especially if you are eighteen when it starts. He had done his time and he was never going back.

Sometimes Mum had surprised him by turning up sober at a random visit, giving him birthday presents from three months earlier. He'd liked those visits. She'd been excited and kept cracking stupid jokes he hadn't heard since he was a kid. He'd loved her then. He'd hated her, but he'd loved her too. Still did.

A couple of cars drove past, but other than that, the industrial area was dead. He guessed they were all indoors, hiding from the weather, wrapping their Christmas presents and drinking *glögg*. It would have to be the variety without alcohol for him this year. It wasn't quite the same but it was good enough. Fishing the almonds and raisins out of the spicy cordial was what he enjoyed the most. He should go and get some gingerbread cookies too.

As the bus pulled up, he straightened his clothes and grabbed the bag. Not a lot of stuff in that bag; he carried enough baggage anyway. He had sent a few things to Mum already, but most of it he'd just left behind. Material possessions weren't his thing. As long as he had his music and his tattered paperbacks he'd be all right.

The bus wound its way through the slush towards Gustav Adolf's *torg*, the place where buses congregate for secret bus meetings, where you can pick a bus at random and end up in a part of the city that you hardly knew existed. But he knew where he was going. The numbers on the bus routes had changed but the routes themselves had stayed the same. The spare key to Mum's flat lay pressed against his leg, like a casino marker, holding the potential for substantial winnings or sore losses. He appreciated the fact that he didn't have to sleep in a hostel, but at the same time he dreaded the sight that waited for him behind the door. He bit his lip and strummed his fingers to the music.

Möllevångstorget hadn't changed. The statue glorifying collective effort was still there, with its people holding a giant boulder. Together. The concept was so alien to him that he spat at it as he walked past.

To save himself the disappointment of coming home and finding the fridge empty, he bought a thick sausage with mash at the Sibylla kiosk and even chose a Coke to go with it. He had never been a big Coke drinker (though rum and Coke had always gone down smoothly) because it had been such a special childhood treat. There had to be a *reason* to drink it. Mum only ever bought lime soda, except on his birthday, when he got to choose.

He smiled to himself. There was a reason to buy Coke today; getting out just in time for the festive season was cool. At least so far. On the side of the kiosk was a poster announcing a New Year's concert in Copenhagen. He could go. He didn't really have the money but he'd be able to scrounge some up. The thoughts lifted him, carried him across the abandoned square to the waiting door, before dropping him like slippery soap in the bath when he discovered that the code to get into the building had finally been changed. Mum hadn't let him know. As he was standing there, staring at the pin pad, trying to think of a reasonable random combination, a young guy with tattoos on his thick neck pressed the pad and entered. Sammi caught the door with his foot and went in. The stairwell had been painted an unusual green since he was last there. It smelt of industrial cleaning liquid and possibly even home baking. Mum had told him there was a new family on the second floor, one with a couple of coloured girls. Bet they were the ones baking. Perhaps Möllevången was turning upmarket now. Mum'd have to move out quick smart if that was the case.

Anyway, time for the real deal, confronting the Mummy Monster in the Haunted House.

The doorbell hadn't worked for as long as he could remember but he knocked a few times and yelled through the mail slot before getting his key out. To step inside was like reliving a dream he'd woken up from years ago. Not that the flat was messy—it wasn't. There weren't enough things to make a mess. On one of her many benders Mum had obviously decided that the minimalist approach was right for her and she'd sold most of the furniture. All that was left was a mattress, a kitchen table with one chair and a staggering number of cushions along the lounge room wall. Books were piled on the floor and in windowsills. He couldn't quite decide if it was an improvement or not. Rather than sitting down on the pile of cushions, he kept moving to check the bathroom (which looked reasonably normal, apart from a battered old poster on the door picturing a fluorescent Jesus with the caption 'I will be your saviour'. In one corner someone had scrawled 'I'm still waiting…').

His old room, on the other hand, was scary. It was as if nothing had changed since the day he last saw it. His bed was unmade. Sammi looked at the sheets. His old ones. Perhaps she hadn't set foot in there for two years.

But it wasn't quite that bad. When he started looking around, he noticed subtle signs of her existence: a couple of coins on the bedside table, a pair of sneakers in the corner, even a vague smell of cigarette smoke tempered with rosewater. He resisted the urge to pocket the coins, then put his bag down next to the bed and walked over to the window. The square below was empty, the way a pocket with a hole is empty, inevitably. The window panes rattled uncomfortably in the raw gale. What was he meant to do now? Sit down and wait for his life to begin? A restlessness that he had grown intimately familiar with was beginning to grab hold of him. A cigarette would help. A drink would make him happy. A pill would loosen all boundaries. But none of the above were options. All he could do was indulge in the thought of them. He lay down on the bed and turned the music up on his Walkman, fantasising about all the girls he had brought home to this bed. It felt like a lifetime ago. Some had stuck in his mind because of a certain way of licking their lips or laughing too loud when he kissed their toes. None of them had visited him inside. To the roaring beat of Rage Against the Machine, he felt himself slipping off to sleep.

When he woke up, the room was dark but there were bustling noises coming from the kitchen. He strained to hear if it was just Mum or several of them. In the old group there had been five: three guys, Mum and another woman called Anita. Anita had been the nice one, slipping him lollies under the table when Mum wasn't looking. Nils-Olof (or N-O as he was called by everyone except Anita) had been all smiles one day and thunder the next. At a visit six months ago, Mum had told him with tears streaming down her face that N-O had been hit by a bus. She'd seen it happen. They'd all been staggering, drunk as always. The bus had just missed her. Sammi had hardly managed to muster up any sympathy for N-O, the old goat, but he felt bad for Mum. For as long as he could remember, that stupid group had been there for her. But she said everything'd changed after N-O's death. They had all felt too guilty to look each other in the eye.

He stood up suddenly and wiped a string of saliva from his cheek with the back of his hand. Whether it happened to be punk rock or opera, it was time to face the music.

'Hi, sweets. Why are you standing there in the dark?' Mum's voice was as familiar as the sound of his own breathing—something you don't realise that you have missed until you hear it again.

'Hi, Mum. I was just on my way to say "hi".'

Her embrace burned through him and, though he tried not to care, he noted that he couldn't smell drink on her breath. Perhaps it would be a nice reunion. Perhaps she had even made them dinner? He tried not to let his thoughts run away with him.

'Sit down!' She motioned to the lone chair. 'I'll get another one from the neighbours.' Before he could stop her, she had twirled out the door and sooner than expected she was back with another chair.

'Sorry about that.' Her grey eyes had a new pattern of wrinkles around them. 'How are you?'

'Good.'

She laughed, throwing her head back to expose her thin neck.

'I'm glad. I'm shit myself but it's nice to know that you're good, my son.'

He laughed too. During his school days, Mum had always been the crazy mum who all the other kids wished was theirs. He had been proud of her then. Her humour was still intact but now he could hear the desperation and loneliness behind her jokes.

'You hungry?'

He thought about it and decided that he was probably ready for more food. She opened the freezer and produced a family sized pizza.

'Your favourite.' She winked at him as she turned the oven on and slid the Hawaiian in.

'Mum, isn't that a bit much for two people? Anyone else coming?'

Even though she was busy getting plates out of the cupboard, she picked up on the anxiety in his voice.

'No, baby, just us.'

Their awkward dance of avoiding any subject that could actually be of interest, such as her group or his life in prison, continued all through the meal. By piecing bits together, he eventually worked out that she had been forced to do a course, any course, to be allowed to keep her social security payments. She had been offered treatment but had refused. She'd chosen to do a gardening course but no job had magically appeared at the end.

'Old bat like me can't change. But you can.'

When she looked at him with that much hope and longing, guilt started gnawing at his stomach. It didn't have to be like that, did it? She could get on the wagon too. There wasn't a limit to the number of sober people in the world, was there? He wanted to reach out to her, hug her and keep her safe, the way she had protected him when he was a kid.

But she hadn't kept him safe, really, had she? He could think of plenty of times when she'd almost managed to kill them both. Like the time she'd fallen asleep with a cigarette burning in her hand and the bed had caught fire, very nearly poisoning them both with putrid smoke. Anita had found them unconscious and called an ambulance. For weeks, the flat had smelt like a bonfire of old tyres gone horribly wrong.

'So, what's next?'

'Suppose I have to find a job. After New Year's probably.'

She looked at him with genuine interest while nibbling on the last piece of pizza.

'What do you want to do?'

It hadn't actually occurred to him that he had a choice in the matter. His entire life he'd always been after simple pleasures, attainable goals: the next drink, an easy fuck, getting out of prison. Quitting had been hard, hellishly hard, probably the hardest thing he'd ever do, so if he could do that, he could do anything, right?

'Maybe something to do with trucks.'

Mum nodded thoughtfully. 'You'd be good at that.'

'Thanks, Mum.'

They lit a few candles and stayed sitting in the kitchen, regaining ground that had been lost to them for a long time. Every half hour, the kitchen clock chimed a few bars from the Beatles' song 'All You Need Is Love'. And every time, they laughed.

✦

Christmas came and went. Sammi bought gingerbread and *glögg*, and it tasted almost as good as he had imagined. One day between Christmas and New Year it began to snow. Large flakes that melted when they hit his face. As the city braced itself for the fireworks extravaganza that was New

Year's Eve, he stood on the balcony and watched the square turn white. Snow put a lid on things, it buried old hatchets and clad the dreary city in its finest frock, ready to party. Standing on the balcony looking down, watching it all unfold below, he imagined himself the way religious nutters imagine God, watching your every move from above. To be a part of the New Year's celebration was almost as impossible as seeing his old friends again. It was easy enough to be all self-righteous, a successful quitter, when you haven't truly been tempted. He'd considered escaping to a cottage in the forest to get away but he didn't know anyone who owned a cottage, and he didn't have a car to get away in even if he found somewhere to go. All he could do was wait, and hopefully he'd make it out unscathed at the other end.

Mum was bustling in the kitchen, actually cooking his favourite meal: roast beef with wedges and béarnaise sauce. He'd almost forgotten that she used to be a great cook when she wasn't drinking. Now she was just quietly sipping a glass of wine and humming 'Ain't No Mountain High Enough'.

'Smells fantastic.'

He resisted the temptation to open the oven door to let more of it out.

'Won't be long now. Why don't you set the table?'

He turned to the cupboard to take out a couple of plates so when it happened, it was in his peripheral vision, barely visible other than a blurry movement just out of reach. There was a slight stumble, a twisted ankle perhaps, something to shrug off, but that was just the beginning. By the time he had let go of the plates and rushed to help her, Mum was already in a heap on the floor, bleeding from a gash to the forehead.

'Fucking hell, Mum. You scared me. You okay?'

Her eyes swam like lost fish in their sockets and she didn't answer. She looked confused rather than scared, with her face sagging like a mask on one side. He didn't want to leave her but he had to step out to the hallway to snatch the phone from the wall to call an ambulance. The seconds away from her were torture. She made little groaning noises when he rushed back.

'They'll be here soon. Don't worry, Mum.'

Choking on his fear, he ran and grabbed the doona from the other room and pulled it over her to keep her warm, a towel from the bathroom to press onto the wound and a glass of water, in case she got thirsty. Then he sat down next to her and held her hand. Looking for changes, touching her cheek, pulling back her grey hair.

The fear of losing her was a runaway truck in the night, coming towards him with blaring horn and burning headlights. She was all he had.

The buzzer from the door downstairs made him jump.

'Come up. Third floor.'

He opened the front door out to the stairs so they wouldn't have to ring again.

'Mum, look at me.'

Her eyes were still unfocused, cloudy, not unlike the day after a big session, but she didn't seem to recognise him.

The paramedics were young, methodical and reassuring. He stepped back and watched as they strapped Mum to a stretcher, answering their questions as well as he could. What had he actually seen? Why had she fallen over?

He fumbled for his jacket and the keys so he could lock the door before heading down the stairs to the ambulance. He didn't really understand how they managed to carry her down the steep flight but he was relieved to see her settled in the ambulance when he got there.

'It'll be fine, Mum. Don't worry. I'm here.'

Her eyes were closed now but he could see her chest moving.

✦

Hours of pacing hospital corridors and eight vending machine chocolates later, a middle-aged woman with deep black hair and piercing blue eyes sat down to tell him what had happened.

'As far as we can see, your mother has had a stroke.'

She paused to let him interject but he kept his mouth shut.

'The stroke probably made her unbalanced and caused the fall. The wound is superficial but the stroke seems to have affected her quite severely.'

'Is she going to die?' He blurted it out, his words coated in fear and injustice.

'No. You did well to ring straight away.'

She was reassuring him like a mother and he hated her for it.

'She has lost a fair bit of movement down her left side, but it might be regained over time.'

'Can I see her?'

She stood up and nodded. 'Of course. Please don't be alarmed if she looks different.'

He followed her down the corridor to a room with three empty beds. In the fourth one was Mum, asleep with her mouth open, grunting and carrying on. Embarrassed for her, he tried to close her mouth. The doctor put a hand on his shoulder.

'Be patient. It might take a while for her to regain her speech and movement.'

So she was a fucking vegetable now? Great. He'd come home just in time to see Mum lose the plot. He shrugged the doctor's hand off.

'Go home and get some sleep.'

Easy for her to say.

He stormed out, tears prickling his eyes. At least it wasn't far to walk home. Midnight had come and gone without him really noticing but everybody else seemed to have had a good time, judging by the fireworks debris littering the footpath and the square. Parties were still playing loud music and the pubs were so full of people that some had spilt out onto the street. That was what New Year's Eve was all about, wasn't it? Hanging out with friends, drinking, flirting. He felt so old, twenty going on a hundred, alone and sober.

As soon as he opened the door, the smell of burnt meat smacked him in the face. He turned off the oven and slid down the wall, resting his head on his knees, trying hard not to crumble. The stench was overpowering and he knew he needed to do something about it but that something eluded him. All his strength had been drained from his body. He hit his head against the wall. Once. Just to see what it was like. Twice. Harder. Three times. His head throbbed but it helped. Four, five, six. He started seeing stars like Donald Duck in the cartoons he'd loved as a kid. Then, beyond the stars, he saw a beacon of light, a glimmering glass with a shiny fluid beckoning him. Mum's wine glass, still brimming, sitting safely on the table. He couldn't reach it. Even as his entire being yearned for a single drop of the elixir of life, he knew that he couldn't touch it. But he needed it so badly. Never in his life had he needed a drink more than right at this moment.

Bullshit. He should stop trying to convince himself that it's okay. It's not. Not a single drop. Ever. He'd be right back where he was.

'Fuck you!' he screamed at no-one in particular, trying to silence the voice in his head. 'Fuck you! What do you know about how I feel? What I need?'

The throbbing in his head grew as he kept banging it

against the wall. Then he changed tactic and started pleading with himself. Hadn't he just had the worst day imaginable? Surely he needed a bit of comfort after all this? He crawled over to the table and grabbed the glass. The Chardonnay smelt sweet as a spring day in an orchard. The wine shimmered. The colour reminded him of that special day when the first leaves unfurl. He closed his eyes and breathed it in. It wasn't too late to stop. He could still put it back on the table and walk away. But the lack of dinner, the sugar overload from eight chocolates, the stench of burnt meat, the banging of his head against the wall—all these factors worked against him. He gripped the glass so tightly that he half expected it to break in his hand. The smell made him dizzy with longing. The moment before he lost his footing and let himself fall, that was the moment, the second, of crystal clear wonder. He stuck his tongue out and licked the rim of the glass before dipping it gently in to feel the prickle of the acid.

Then he closed his eyes and drank, poured the entire glass down his throat, the way others pour water over plants in the garden, recklessly. He threw the empty glass against the wall, where it broke into a constellation of shards at the same moment the kitchen clock started playing 'All You Need Is Love'.

---

**Anna Solding's** first novel *The Hum of Concrete* was nominated for six awards, including the Commonwealth Bank Prize, Most Underrated Book Award and People's Choice Award. Anna earned her Masters and PhD in Creative Writing from the University of Adelaide. She works as managing director at MidnightSun Publishing and enjoys making Swedish chocolate balls.

# A Paper Woman

Melanie Kinsman

Before you came I spent a bitter winter. My heart froze in my chest. The hospital sheets lay thin and flat against my ribcage. My breasts had been cut off and a slash of a scar lay in their place. I slept with the television on, so the sound would drown out my loneliness. Black and white plumes engulfed me, and its glow burned away the dark.

I was single, twenty-three and living on my own. I had no lover to please and no child to feed. A pair of breasts wasn't much to sacrifice in the face of death. In the mirror I saw the dark eyes of a Jew in a camp. My face was hollow from starvation.

An age passed while I slept. I woke and found myself feeling disembodied: a pile of bones, a wreath of dusty hair, a loose jaw, a pair of teeth. These fragments struggled to work in unison. My hands shook when they held a cup. I wet myself like an infant. I was no longer sure who I was. Perhaps I did not even know who I had been. Remnants of the past did not seem to matter. My body was not my own: it was a gutted shell attached to an IV and a heart monitor. The heart monitor had a filament that bore into my chest. It tracked each beat with a soft ping, reassuring me that my heart was steady, but my ears rang with phantom sirens.

Yet I lived. Tenuously but steadily, I lived. As I healed,

I lay within the hospital walls like a baby in a humidicrib, catching only fleeting glimpses of the world beyond. My window revealed the tops of ragged palm trees. I saw street-lamps and heard the noises of traffic, but I forgot everything else outside: dinners with friends, trips to the beach, motion pictures. The newspaper headlines said that Egypt had fallen and there was civil war in Syria. This crisis was remote, far from my bed; I could not hear the noise of war and revolution. Even the simplest of things, like choosing what clothes to wear each day, became the memories of someone else. The sky and the sun and the earth moved, but my world had dissolved into the trivial and the mundane—the vague thrill of lunch and dinner arriving on a tray.

For a while I was weakened by the operation and dependent on machines. Things that had once been ordinary became achievements. I learned to walk around with an IV on a mobile pole. My catheter was removed, and I was able to urinate in a toilet. Later, when I walked down the corridor unshackled, I saw the views from other windows. I saw drain pipes and gutters, asphalt, trees and rubbish bins. With each new glimpse of the world, I was reminded of its enormity. I was a bird in a box: a flurry of feathers, a frantic heartbeat. I was young and in hospital, on a macabre vacation from my own life.

I left. I fled with a bare chest. I was a fledgling woman: unmade, unfinished, an amputee. The surgeon had cut off my nipples and removed my breast tissue. I did not ask for a reconstruction. The thought of saline implants inflating on my chest like the air bags of a car frightened me. The surgeon suggested replacing the missing tissue with half of my shoulder muscle. He wanted to attach it to my chest. This feat of engineering came at a price—I would have a weak shoulder for the rest of my life. The surgeon didn't seem to care. He was excited by his plastic possibilities. *Don't worry, nipples are easier to make,* he said. *I can make them from your vaginal flesh.*

These man-made parts horrified me. I imagined them as the body parts of another, crudely sewn onto my chest. They seemed no better than the monstrous work of a 19thcentury surgeon who wanted to hack off gangrenous legs and attach wooden stumps.

In the end I did the only thing I could do. I threw away my bras, so I would not be tempted to stuff them, and despite the constant stares at my flat chest, I did nothing.

I returned to my creative arts degree. The university was a place of great promise, filled with bright young things. I wanted to be like these bright young things. I wanted to argue the merits of Ulysses over a beer at the tavern on Friday afternoons. Yet I could never be as carefree as they were, hard as I tried. Drinking and partying could not make me forget that my time at the university was transient. I'd already seen the end in a ward full of demented, white-haired women, dying as the smell of boiled mutton drifted in from the kitchen.

But then there was you. You took the same writing class that I did. You smiled at me. The amusement in your eyes was brazen. It was a challenge, but I could not meet your gaze. I was wafer-thin, pale, and nervous. I spent a semester waiting for the moments when you spoke in class, and I listened to every word you said. I noticed that you had white, middle-class teeth, but one crooked tooth objected, making your smile imperfect. The rest of your face was harder to read. It was lined in a way that made it difficult to tell if you were twenty or forty. You were ageless and if life had shown you any grievances, you had weathered them well.

You had lived another life before coming to university.

It had been an unlikely one, with steps out of time, like my own; you were once a *wunderkind*, a child actor on a television show. You were famous enough to be recognised, but not famous or rich enough for ruin. A career before university made you wise in the ways of the world; the bitterness of unemployment left its aftertaste in your mouth. Yet you were like the other bright young things in ways I could never be: you knew nothing of illness, nothing of rehydrated mash on a dinner tray at five o'clock. You lined your stomach with vodka and smoked cigarettes until three a.m. You squinted like James Dean. You were irreverent. You drew cartoons. Your hair was dyed a furious orange. Your clothes had holes. You risked everything for a laugh, and if a joke fell flat or went too far, you didn't care.

I was afraid to do anything that drew attention. I hid among the flocks of my girlfriends at parties, shielding myself from the eyes of men. I watched you from within. Your recklessness was compelling, and I was fascinated and envious.

As the semester went by, these parties became indistinguishable. Girls preened, boys wrestled, everybody got drunk. I watched and you waited. Nothing changed until I sat next to you at the end-of-semester pub crawl. You were lying on a couch, smoking a blunt and looking completely relaxed. I felt dramatically nervous. People were trying to shout over the music of the DJ. You reached over and took my arm, as if it was the most natural thing in the world. I waited for you to speak, but you didn't say anything. On the street outside I asked how high you were. You shrugged and said it did not matter.

We ate a late night kebab on a city street. I hailed a taxi at three a.m. and you followed me into it. You said you were going in the same direction. You were house-sitting somewhere on the city fringe. You were deliberately vague. Your stop was earlier than mine, but you got out at my house. It was cold and mist had formed around the trees on the street.

*You have made a mistake*, I said, thinking of my cavernous chest. *You had better go on with the taxi. You can't come in.*

*That's all right*, you said. *We can talk here. You'll have to lend me a jumper, though. It's freezing.*

Lending you clothing was a challenge. You were tall and your shoulders were broad. I was five feet with the frame of a sparrow. I went into the house and returned with the biggest thing I had, which was a faded yellow bathrobe with a bit of stretch. You took the robe and wrapped it around your shoulders, unfazed by your appearance.

We stood under the trees for two hours and talked. You did not ask to come in. At dawn you said you had to go. You had to tend to the cat at the house you were minding. The cat was demented and senile, but the owners could not bear to put it down. They insisted that you prise its jaws open and force a pill down its throat each morning, an act that denied its decrepitude, and was difficult for you to perform without injury. I laughed loudly as you pretended to suppress an indignant cat with your hands.

*Little brute cries most of the night*, you said. *You have saved me from its wretched companionship.*

You didn't try to kiss me like I expected you to. You didn't try any of the things young men often did on dates: claim me with greedy hands, fumble for a feel, stick a hot tongue in my ear. You had made me laugh and were satisfied with that. You said goodnight and wished me well. You seemed bemused and your words were gentle.

The university holidays began. I did not see you. There were no classes, and you did not call. I wondered what would have happened if I had let you into my house. I agonised over your last words to me. I questioned your motives. Perhaps you had been playing with me for your own entertainment. Perhaps the whole night had been nothing more to you than a silly adventure with some girl. By the end of the holidays I was convinced you would never speak to me again.

But you did. The new semester began. During classes you watched me intently. Your eyes never left me. I wondered what you saw. You said that you saw a woman with coffee skin and a generous mouth; someone with a long neck and a dark crown of curls. In my eyes I was still a hospital patient, worn out like old thread.

The first time you saw me naked, I was afraid. I had not warned you of the scar. I quivered before you in the room, raw and unclad, afraid of disgust and shock in your eyes. I was a paper woman, thin and flammable. Your gaze was a match.

When you smiled at me I saw wisdom older than the years on your face. Your eyes were the colour of slate. I saw a glimpse of your crooked tooth. You cradled my ribs in your hands. You rubbed your cheeks against mine with a raw, animal delight, like a primate looking into a mirror and poking at its reflection.

Night after night your hands mapped my face. Your rusty, earthy smell seeped into my sheets. We spent the summer drinking and smoking marijuana. We watched B-movies from the 1950s and read each other stories from the newspaper. We discussed communism and photography.

During university lectures you drew caricatures of Tony Abbott and Julia Gillard wringing each other's necks; Julia's pointy nose and Tony's jug ears appeared in the margins of my notes on Gothic novels. After university we went to cheap vegetarian restaurants and drank homebrew beer. We collected vintage lounge chairs for your apartment, trawling op shops full of the debris of past lives. For every vinyl chair in mint condition there was a discarded Tupperware set, or a pair of sensible socks that had never been unwrapped, mean in their own cheapness. But despite collecting things from the recently dead, I did not think of the hospital, or dwell on the weeks I'd spent within its walls. I was out in the world, listening for news of the Syrian civil war, eating eggs hollandaise for breakfast, seeing the sights from the windows of your car.

When it got too hot to drive around we sat in the vintage chairs, holding spray bottles and damp cloths in our laps. We pulled down the blinds of the windows and lived in semi-darkness, venturing out to go to university and drink beer in the tavern. You worked part-time as a clown at children's parties to pay the rent. I played house, making cakes from scratch and writing our university papers.

The hot weather dragged into March. I began to feel hollow. I was a babushka doll made of cheap wooden shells, slowly unfolding as parts of me broke down and disappeared. My hair stopped growing. My gums began bleeding. My voice became a rasp.

I stopped drinking and staying up late. You carried me to bed instead of keeping me awake all night, wrangling about with me in the sheets. You brought me cups of hot milk. You watched over me with the patience and concern of a new mother, but all your attention was not enough. One afternoon, when you were making balloon animals at a party, I passed out in the flat. When I woke there was an ambulance crew in the bedroom. I sat up and roared at you, outraged that you had called 000. You looked at me with a pained expression. I had been unconscious and you had not been able to rouse me.

I was taken to hospital in the ambulance. I was strapped to machines and filled with antibiotics. The doctor put a tube into my chest and administered medicine through a line, which my heart pumped to my arteries. Within an hour I could sit up. I felt re-energised, like a pressed flower that had fallen out of the pages of a book and into water, a dried husk filled with life.

I wanted to go back to the flat. The doctor advised against it. He insisted I sign a 'Discharged Against Medical Advice' form. You intervened to end a stand-off. You knew I would be difficult to persuade. *Do not go gentle into that good night*, you said, quoting Dylan Thomas, raising your hand and pretending to skol a bottle of wine. You stumbled around for comic effect. I laughed, and I stayed.

So did you. The nurses wheeled a trundle bed into the room for you. I lay next to you all night. My skin withered from my bones; fragments of paper fell. I listened to the sounds of your deep breathing. I did not need the drone of television advertising to fight off the emptiness of the night. When I felt afraid I put my head in the hollow under your neck, like a child clutching its mother's chest.

The next day you wheeled me out of the ward and into the hospital gardens. I closed my eyes against the glare of the sun. Loud noises seemed to hurt my ears. I could not eat the fried chicken you had brought for me; anything beyond the bread of hospital food tasted foreign. I was afraid to be outside the hospital walls, like a prisoner released into a crowd after years of solitary confinement.

I did not fear a lack of consciousness. It had happened once, and it would happen again. I wanted nothing for myself. I thought about the women you would sleep with after me. I wanted to tell you this did not matter.

*Ten years from now you will have a wife,* I said. *I will be a girl that died before you met.* You did not want to listen. You were like the other bright young things, and had enough youthful arrogance to ignore me.

Yet this was enough. You saved me. You raised me from the ashes. I was a small mound on a cliff, waiting to be blown away into the wind. I felt your hands on me as my consciousness flickered like a faltering light. I closed my eyes and listened to your voice, ageless and eternal as the lines already etched into your face. I held on to the moment, and to you, for as long as I could.

---

**Melanie Kinsman** has a PhD in Creative Writing from the University of Adelaide. She was shortlisted for the Overland Short Story Prize in 2012, and has co-edited a collection of short stories published by Wakefield Press.

# Something About Religion

Reg Taylor

The new minister was tall and dark and stern-looking but once he'd unloaded his family and the foster girl they brought with them he got stuck straight into his parish duties and people who'd been involved with the church for years reckoned he was a breath of fresh air.

To begin with, I don't think my brother Richard and I cared much; church was a kind of torture. We didn't expect to be relieved. It was only when the minister decided to put a broom through the choir and make us join our mother and sister in it that we sat up and took notice. It was bad enough having to wade through Communion every Sunday, counting down the pages left in the prayer book and getting ready to dig our father in the ribs if he tried to sing; we treasured the two spare evenings a week when our mother and sister were out and we could roam the town and explore buildings still empty from the 1956 Flood.

Yet from the first night of choir practice we became converts; with a little direction we soon learned to take on any musical hurdle put in our paths; from the moment we put on our cassocks on Sundays we knew what it was like to be part of a select and jealous band.

I liked to think that our father, left to stoically grunt his responses on his own in church after that, might have taken some pride in his son's contribution to the service and felt less inclined to join in himself. But then I was never really sure where he stood when it came to religion. I don't think he ever looked too deeply into the Divine, or was troubled by a spiritual crisis or the thoughts of Retribution that used to sometimes wake me in the small hours of the morning, wishing I could put off the day. I think he saw church almost in sporting us-against-them denominational terms—except when it came to the Catholics, of course, who were serious competitors with the Church of England for the lion's share of the town's spiritual spoils.

The Lutherans hardly rated in Renmark, incidentally, even though in Loxton on the other side of the River you could hardly move for them. When a new girl, Karen, turned up halfway through Grade Six with a German surname and said her father was the new pastor I almost wondered whether she was some kind of refugee from over there. There was definitely nothing Krautish about her. Loxton's big raw-boned footballers used to fill us with dread when they took the field, but she was small and demure looking and had a grown up air that gave real grown-ups the confidence to dump responsibilities on her.

Looks could be misleading, though. While she was sitting in class with her arms folded and her feet tucked under her she might look like Grace Kelly in *High Noon*, but it was different when she was making a dive for the ball on the netball court or screaming for someone to pass it to her. She'd do almost anything for a dare too—even if, to be honest, it sometimes seemed like she could get away with almost anything: teachers hardly ever told her off. I know being good at school helped—when she came in late and said, 'I'm sorry Miss Combey, but I really wanted to finish this'—while she was handing over something that you knew would be the best in class (and not only because it was coming up against the efforts of kids whose idea of illustrating a project on Switzerland was to stick in a picture of a couple of tins of Carnation milk)—what was the teacher going to say?

But there was something else about her that seemed to make even grown-ups wary of rubbing her up the wrong way. One of the girls in class lived in a shack out on the flats at Paringa with a father who had three cows and a TPI pension and called himself a dairy farmer, and she used to come to school smelling of cow shit and get picked on until Karen stuck up for her one day. 'Leave her *alone!*' she screamed in some fatso's face and no one went near her after that.

Since she was so tough it made the time she got sick and missed weeks of school, disturbing. It was while she was away that the headmaster decided to start up weekly marching lessons, and I used to think of Karen with sympathy—and some envy too, since I enjoyed being sick so much myself—lying in bed on those days at her home near the school; spared the humiliation of being involved in what was happening in the quadrangle (though even if she'd been well I think she'd have found some way of getting out of it) and laying down her copy of *Little Women* or *Girls' Own Annual* as the music drifted across to her; immune to it but in some way still appreciative of my concern. The day she came back to school I brimmed with anticipation—that some little tell-tale couldn't wait to overturn: 'He'—the tell-tale hissed sarcastically as we filed into class—'is so glad to see you again. He just couldn't *wait*…' I felt myself reddening, waiting for the axe that always fell at times like that. But all Karen said was, 'I know'—without breaking stride, and with just enough stress on the first word to wipe the smirk off the other little smarty's face.

After that we were said to be 'going' with one

another—even though we never went anywhere: it wasn't allowed. Once we got as far as meeting up at the pictures, which was risky enough, sitting with just the aisle between us. At half time I bought her a Hi-Top which she nibbled lady-likely, but afterwards we had to sit through a really bad choice for a Saturday matinee while a couple of hundred other kids booed and whistled and stamped their feet so hard that whole rows of seats rocked. When we met up outside in the hard afternoon light that always gave me a headache I apologised, but she insisted, 'I always like Audrey Hepburn,' before she and her friend hurried home to have tea with an aunty.

That afternoon mightn't have been a success, but there were other times. On Guy Fawkes' night we got involved in a game on the Paringa Oval just out of reach of parents' eyes and in the glow of bonfires and fireworks. She looked elated then. At school you had to be more careful; one day when we were trailing the rest on some walk Miss Combey looked back and said drily, 'The rest of us will just wait while Mum and Dad catch up.' You wouldn't want to get caught holding hands. We had to make do with sitting across from each other on the corner of the sandpit at lunchtime while Karen had a book out and we talked about what we were going to be when we grew up.

I used to look for her face every day when I came in.

✦

One day in early December the whole school was taken to the pool in town. It was really only done as a way of filling in time after the exams, but the headmaster still made sure it was all organised. We were divided up into teams so we could cheer on our instant heroes plodding up and down the pool. I ran out of steam in a relay and finished up having to dog paddle the last few yards, which was better than some weakies who had to be hauled out bawling after they panicked in the six-foot end, but Karen had a note from home excusing her and her Speedos from even getting wet. It was unseasonably cool; the tail end of some system from up north had overshadowed the event with drizzle and cloud. She was never a great pool person anyway, only going in on really hot days and then she'd hardly get her hair wet as she did a crossing or two in breast stroke before she got out and tucked her bathers back under her and covered her shoulders with a towel. She tactfully avoided mentioning my efforts but she still looked restless. 'What shall we *do*…?' she sighed, frowning in the direction of the pool.

'We're not allowed out of here,' I reminded her.

'Oh, pooh—who'd know?' She got up and pivoted on one hip. 'Show us your church. You're always talking about it.'

It was only just down the street and I'd boasted I knew where the back door key was—'I can go in whenever I like'—even though I'd actually only used it once when I helped Mum change the flowers. We had to make a show of splitting up before we got to the park outside the pool, but once we were in the clear Karen hooked my arm in hers and scrunched up alongside. '*See*'—she teased, 'bad luck I left my high heels home'—and she stayed chirpy until we got closer to the church and had to sneak around the river side of the building.

She stared whispering then: 'You're sure there'll be no one there?' but once we were inside she perked up again. 'Gorgeous'—she said stagily when she saw the altar laid out in purple for Advent, and when I pointed to the stalls where the choir sat she said, 'I bet you look sweet.' Then she looked at the door down at the end of the main aisle. 'What's through there?'

'Not much'—I started to tell her about the vestry but she was already heading that way. She looked back and raised her eyebrows at the door before she slipped through it, but then she showed up again only a second or two later and just about galloped back with the floorboards bounding under her. '*Come on!*' she said, and as we were scrambling back outside she hissed in my ear, 'There was someone *there!*'

I was fumbling with the key. 'Who?'

'I don't know—a man with glasses.'

'Did he see you?'

'I don't think so. There was a big girl in there with him.'

'What were they doing?'

She almost choked. '*You* know…'

I didn't really. There was a girl in class who used to spend half her time with the boys, probably because the other girls didn't want her around, and one day she smirked to us, 'You can always tell when Mum and Dad are *doing* it—you can hear their bed squeaking.' But she was the sort of girl who'd have parents like that. After Karen and I got outside we were like partners who'd come adrift in a three legged race; by the time I looked back from seeing if the coast was clear she'd left me for dead. The last thing she threw back over her shoulder at me was, 'What'd you have to take me in *there* for?' and by the time I got to the pool she was with her team and pretending to be interested in what was happening in the water.

The next day at school she still didn't want to know me so I gave her the same treatment and we didn't speak for the last couple of weeks of term.

The day of our break-up party Miss Combey was unwrapping her presents when she asked for a volunteer to cover up the sick someone had left on the steps outside. I'd just managed to make it back with a bucket load of sand from the sandpit and dump it in front of the kid sitting there with his head between his knees, when Karen came out.

'Yuk,' she said and gave the mess a wide berth, but then she followed me to the troughs in the shelter shed and stood behind me while I was washing my hands. I dragged it out until she got fed up.

'Guess what?' she said.

I didn't turn around, I just said, 'What.'

'I won't be here next year.'

'Why not?'

'We're going to live in Loxton. Dad's been made pastor of the big church over there.'

'Well what's it got to do with me?' I said. I decided to let her have it. 'What'd you have to blame me for what happened in church that day anyway—how was I supposed to know?'

'Oh…' She shrugged, and looked around as if she was worried some big-ears might be listening. 'Do you want to know something else?'

'I suppose.'

She twisted. 'It's…because of something that happened when I was little, that's why…'

'What?'

'Oh'—she made out she was trying to be patient. 'It was when we were at the other church in Nuri—there was a man there one day, a friend of Dad's, when there was no church on. I was just playing out the front and he asked me to let him in…he made out he wanted me to show him something…'

'So?'

She looked around and then over towards the classroom. 'Well, when we got inside he—he touched me—and he showed me his thing…That's all.' When she turned back her fists were closed on her chest and her eyes were wet. 'He made me promise not to tell, so don't you either.'

I knew I wouldn't. I didn't even want to know about her being interfered with.

'Anyhow,' she said, 'I don't have to wait till the bell goes. Mum's picking me up early to go shopping at Hambours. Old Combey said I could go.' She took a small step that brought her right up to me. 'I'm not worried about the other kids. Only you.'

I was shocked by the soft feel of her lips; all our aunties left you feeling like you'd been scrubbed with violets. She just smelt of skin.

'See you,' she said. 'Mum's come.'

✦

Sometimes over the holidays I imagined things like Karen's father changing his mind and moving back to Renmark, or Karen giving her parents such a hard time that they'd let her come and board with someone in Renmark. But, really, I knew it wouldn't happen. Loxton was more than ten miles away and you had to catch the punt to get there… In the New Year we actually made a trip over there when Mum was in some classical concert they put on at Easter in the Lutheran church. It was a massive place after what we were used to, a monument to German pioneers so they said; quarried out of local limestone with an upstairs organ and it could hold five hundred people. Even if Karen had made it—and I think her mother went more for things like 'The Sound of Music'—she'd have been lost in that crowd. Then, when the football season started we went there again with some other kids to see Renmark get done by Loxton (as usual) and that only reminded me that if she followed the football she'd most likely have been barracking for Loxton by then. I knew from us moving around so much that loyalties didn't last long.

And then we had Confirmation coming up. Twice a week my brother and I had to go after school with half a dozen other kids for classes in church. You weren't allowed to muck around—when we were being shown how to line up for Communion and someone donged their head on the rail the Reverend's glasses glittered: 'This is a solemn business,' he warned us. One day he asked if any of us would like to be altar boys when we finished. It didn't look bad fun; you just had to stand out the front and pass the minister things and look a bit reverent. Then Dad surprised us by telling us what his Confirmation was like: 'I got a feeling, almost like an electric shock, passing down from the Bishop's hands,' he said. That gave us something to look forward to.

But before that the Rector got up in church one day and told everyone right out of the blue he was leaving. Dad said, 'Oh well, they must have needed him to fill the breach somewhere else,' but he was disappointed. Even if the monthly meetings of the men's group the minister had started finished up with nothing more than a collective clearing of charred throats before the minister's wife came home and opened every window in the house, Dad never missed one. 'Give him his due, too,' Dad said, 'when that girl they were fostering got herself in the family way—messing about with some coot—he showed her the door quick smart.' I had a picture of the girl getting her marching orders from the minister, with his wife and children giving her the glare from behind him, but she'd never been much more than a top heavy presence round the church, anyway, with a vacant sort of look that Mum thought might have been adenoidal.

Something more serious happened about that time anyway. Richard's voice and then mine broke and that was the end of our involvement with any choir. We had to go back and join our father in the body of the church. And then at our Confirmation in November in the stifling church all I felt under the Archbishop's touch was a trickle of sweat easing its way down to join the pools under my new nylon shirt.

✦

I don't know if it was especially hot that year but right up until school started we went with our mother when she visited Babies Clinics and we had a dip every day in a different town.

Some of the places had proper swimming pools and some didn't. Loxton didn't, but there was a fenced off part on the river for smaller kids and a diving board facing the river on the edge of it for people who felt like trying their luck in the main stream, and once you got used to the musty smell and taste and not being able to see when you were under, the river was never that bad.

We only went in for half an hour on the day we were there because there was a matinee on at the pictures, so we missed what happened after we left. We were sitting waiting in the car at the hospital while our mother was inside collecting something when an ambulance screamed up the drive and three or four grown-ups jumped out and ran past us. You could tell from their panicky look and the colour of the kid they were carrying that something bad must have happened. She had bathers on.

When I was five I nearly drowned in Lake Bonney. It gave me something to boast about; other kids couldn't: every year some toddler or other used to wander away from whoever was minding them and be found floating in one of the local irrigation channels. Once, just after we'd started school, a new teacher got a bit cocky trying to swim across Katarapto

Creek and once, too, I remember, a kid from Renmark Primary drowned on one of the sandbars near Renmark on a Sunday afternoon. His older brother still came to school the next day, but I remember him wandering around looking lost at lunchtime.

We had to wait for the news that night to hear what happened, and for the *Murray Pioneer* to bring the whole story out later in the week. The drowning made the front page because it was local but also because of the way the girl died. The story praised her up, saying that even though she wasn't a strong swimmer, when some kid dived off the big board and got into trouble she went straight in—and then got dragged under herself before anyone else helped out. After all that the other kid finished up being saved, but it was more than quarter of an hour before they managed to find her. There was stuff in there about her being an exemplary student; active in sport, popular with her classmates—those who didn't get on the wrong side of her, I'll bet—and a photo.

You could still tell who it was, but even if it had only been a year or so since I'd seen her, she looked different; her face seemed longer and sort of watchful. I'm not quite sure why it's come to mind now, but at the time it seemed to help. It distanced her, and it still does when I think of it, even while it makes me wonder how much more she might have changed if she'd lived. I know there are some things that don't alter in people, that they can only cover up or put aside, but thinking of that photo I wonder if it might have been the last chance for the old Karen—sitting there with her first lot of pimples, maybe—to just dive in without thinking when that kid sang out.

You can make too much of things. After my mother

fished me out of Lake Bonney she said, 'God couldn't have been quite ready for you,' which for years I thought meant I'd been saved for something special. Now I know that if I had drowned that day the sun wouldn't even have blinked.

I still think of her, Karen, sometimes though, if only for when her 'I know' shut that other kid up at school. It was like she had a secret, a nice one, she wasn't going to let anyone spoil. It's sad to think that after all that we could have both been at the River at the same time that day and not known about it—or known each other...think of that. But I'm glad I wasn't among the crowd when she was so forsaken.

---

**Reg Taylor's** submission for a PhD in Creative Writing at the University of Adelaide in 2014 included a novel, *Landfall,* based on the lives of some of those involved in the New Australia settlement in Paraguay in the 1890s.

# Whatever Happened to the Fairytale Ending?

Mary Lynn Mather

You wake to the unfamiliar sound of birds twittering. For a few seconds, you wonder if it is dusk or dawn, caught in that twilight zone that could be either. As your eyes adjust to the gloom, the surroundings are revealed in grey relief: the curve of her crib, the row of teddy bears on the toy box, the cupboard a solid rectangle in the corner.

She has let you lie in for the first time in weeks. You rest against the nest of pillows and cushions. A grateful sigh slips from your lips. Arms stretch with a life of their own and your thoughts follow, going nowhere in particular.

The blanket weighs you down and you kick your feet free, picturing how she churns chubby legs when you dress her, jerking her limbs in joyous circles. Milk leaks from your breasts and you smell sour dampness on the sheets. A car screams around the corner, reminding you of the accident that happened a few days after her birth, when a truck crashed into the fence of the house next door and you did not stir. Your incredulous husband told all your friends about it, grinning broadly with each repetition of the anecdote and you marvelled at it too, amazed at how motherhood breeds selective hearing.

'It was so weird,' he kept saying. 'The woman who jumps out of bed the instant the baby starts to niggle managed to sleep through this loud bang, the neighbours' shrieks and the ambulance siren. Sweetie, you were dead to the world.'

'Typical,' you retorted. 'You're able to get up for a bit of drama but you can't change a wet nappy at 3am.'

'Touché,' he replied, hugging you and laughing. 'Guilty as charged.'

He is already busy in the kitchen. There is the chink of glass against wood, the thump of a pot on the stove, the soft hiss and gurgle of the coffee percolator. He is tidying the worst of the mess before he has his shower and drives to the office.

Perhaps you should pad across the mat, take in the exquisite scent of her and bring her back to the warm bed. You glance in her direction and marvel at the stillness. It seems a pity to break the spell, so you surrender to inactivity, enjoying the lull in the routine.

You press your exhausted body into the mattress as you used to do at the end of yoga classes, sinking into the corpse pose. You miss the sense of wellbeing you found at those sessions, so you resolve to start practising your basic asana during her midday naps. You suspect you have not been paying enough attention to your marriage and you vow to hire a sitter while the two of you go out for dinner. You decide to rediscover gardening and knitting, hobbies that defined your existence before her arrival, and you look forward to pruning the tangled rosebushes and retrieving the spinning wheel from the shed.

✦

The sun has slunk across a section of the floor. Her cot is still in a pool of darkness but the book of fairytales is illuminated. You must have dropped off again. All is quiet, apart from the hum of the washing machine as it shuffles through its daily cycle. You feel a chill of apprehension, as cold as a curse. She should have demanded to be fed hours ago and you long for the indignant wail. Panic flips your stomach as you rush across the room, tripping over his briefcase. He calls out, asking if you are okay.

In repose, she is like an angel, her face pale and serious, as if she is concentrating. In a daze, you watch for the fluttering of her tiny chest. You lean your ear towards the bud of her mouth.

'Peter, I don't think she's breathing!'

He is in the doorway within seconds, holding a spatula up like a wand. Fear pins him there, unable to cross the threshold.

'Oh, Belle.' You hear your voice, calm and detached, coming from somewhere else. It seems a hundred years old.

---

For much of her life, **Mary Lynn Mather** has scribbled down wild ideas and thrown them into boxes. Many are emerging in the experimental novel she is crafting. She enjoys playing with narrative perspectives. When not trying to reconcile four different stories, Mary Lynn reads plenty of literary fiction.

# The Abduction of Ganymede

Gay Lynch

> *The male human is beautiful when his cheeks are still smooth, his body hairless, his head full-maned, his eyes clear, his manner shy and his belly flat.*
>
> Germaine Greer, *The Boy*

You rest your arm on the balustrade of stairs leading to the railway concourse while checking your phone app for the platform number and departure time of the train to Freo. You hear the tapping of rubber shoes on the black filigreed metal steps, a whoosh of air that flaps like clothing or wings and smells of perspiration and fried food. Someone cannons into you from behind. As you fall, you half turn, to see a thin boy using his arm like a paddle in turbulent waters to shore you up against the rail. You gasp at his face. At the piece of red leather tied around his hairless neck; at the tatty lace scarf veering to one side during the collision. At his beauty.

His full lips tremble, his eyes dart across your face and away as if in terror of a commuter in a silk shirt calling a transit guard. Or the police. Panic travels across his soft childish face. You want to press your thumb against the cleft in his tilted chin, like the god who placed it there.

When he sees you swaying in the right direction, he retracts his arm and pulls his too-small, dirty-green jacket across his chest, sweeps his fingers through shaggy fronds of yellow hair as a girl his age might do, shakes a bracelet of threaded plastic seeds down his arm to his wrist. He looks about thirteen.

Next he splays two uncertain fingers in a V against his lips and gasps as if he's been hurt before and he thinks you, not he, effected this collision, exposing him to danger. You feel his indecisive breath on your neck, before he leaps past you onto the platform. As he rounds a newstand, he swings back to look at you, his face pink and parchment-gold against the green of his collar, like an angel boy in the morning light.

Curving your hand round the flesh at your side, you draw in a sharp painful breath, registering an abrasion that may stain the only article of clothing remaining after a week of all-day conference-going and long boozy dinners. In fact, you had been wearing the shirt the previous night when, in the pursuit of knowledge and under the influence of Benedictine, you had kissed a postdoc not much younger than you in a taxi on its way to Miss Maud's Swedish Hotel. Such irony that his semen had not so much flown like tap-water but damned up when he passed out—before you had chanced to read his three-line bio.

The swell of morning commuters nudges you forward, gathers you up and you surge along with them. Before you reach the row of carriages and step up into the third, you glance at the signed route: City West; West Leederville; Subiaco; Daglish; Shenton Park; Karrakata; Loch Street; Claremont; Swanbourne; Grant Street, Cottlesloe; Mosman; North Fremantle; Fremantle (18.7 km). You like trains—their tetchy engines, their hissing doors, the steep drop beneath the carriages to the rails, signalling your strange fear of jumping, not of falling. You push past a girl with ear phones threaded through her spiky absinthe-coloured hair, playing a game on her phone and past a middle-aged man reading a Manga comic, to take the only empty seat, on a bench that runs between the luggage corral and the door.

At first you don't notice the beautiful boy, clutching at vertical yellow poles to counteract the weight of his back-pack; creeping past you like a Manna crab, heading towards the far wall of the carriage as if pursued by demons; sliding down the wall at the end of the carriage; hunkering down over his cracked running shoes. He doesn't appear to notice you at all as he twirls the end of his lacy scarf. Well good.

You open Germaine Greer's *The Boy* to a page of text, feeling like a paedophile. Then glance around to make sure that no-one observes you flicking past Proem with its disturbing elongated illustration, to a page comprising only text. 'Adolescence is not a moment but a process. A male child becomes a boy when it starts but may not yet be a man when it finishes,' Greer asserts. Surely it is different, as close to actra-fraternal as you can get, for an art academic to view a photograph showing a boy's penis, compared to the way a voyeur might: dreaming of power? After all, you are about to meet a researcher in the field of Neoplatonic readings of the male nude—in more neutral circumstances. After the meeting you'll go with him to a gallery that serves decent food and coffee, to renegotiate your criticism of his paper.

The boy on the floor begins to weep in a soft quiet way using his sleeve to cover his face but you can tell. Should you say something? It's probably nothing to do with the small bump he gave you on the stairs. He cannot realise how vulnerable he looks, how much he invites undesirable attention. You sit up straighter, try to flick him a rueful smile as if to say 'you're alright… I'm alright…Cheer up,' but he doesn't appear to notice you at all. Not now or until he mowed you down. You cross your bare legs. Apart from the small abrasion and a fright, you have come to no harm. Sunshine warms the back of your neck through the window.

At the next stop, more passengers exit than climb aboard. The boy remains crunched over his bag on the floor refusing eye contact. Why does he not pull himself together and take a seat? But he is not your responsibility, any more than the poststructuralist who fell asleep in your bed last night.

✦

At Subiaco Station, two bare-chested youths of sixteen or so, wait on the platform scrunching their white tee shirts in front of them. You know nothing more about Subiaco than last week's television footage of transit guards beating unconscious pumped-up spectators from the nearby stadium. You see no resemblance between these two youths and AFL initiates. One drags behind the other in a khaki military-style jacket with epaulettes. One looks sleepy, the other nervy. Their torsos are pale and lean; their thigh muscles show little definition beneath denim jeans sagging at half-mast. Rocking against each other as they leap into the carriage, they manage to stay upright, their searchlight eyes tracking back and forth across the aisle, seeking anyone blocking their access, before they subside on the seat opposite you.

In the warmth of the carriage, the smaller one with a thin, pointy face—ratty would be too unkind for he is pretty in an unvarnished way—slumps on the seat, one arm draped across the rise of his belly, long slim fingers dangling, head nodding on his skinny chest. He elbows his mate in the ribs. 'Kasimir. Kasi.'

The other starts, an aggrieved look on his face. 'What the fuck?' He dabs at a smear of blood from a mouth pleated with anxiety and wrings water out of his shirt onto the upholstery.

They confer.

'I don't give a fuck, Ethan,' he says.

You can't follow their conversation about not getting enough, and when it went in, and fantasy, but you know they aren't talking about Harry Potter. That they're off their faces on something. You glance uneasily around the carriage trying not to meet their eyes, still shielding the illustrations in Greer's book with your hand.

The taller one, Kasi, stares directly at you. Holds your gaze in an aggressive way. You close the book. He has handsome Slavic features: strong dark eyebrows that meet across his long nose, deep-set brown eyes, a wide mouth and a fine curly hair sprouting at his throat. He has pushed decent imitation designer sunglasses into his dark hair.

Next, he stares across the space to *your* boy and points him out to his mate.

Prickles run down your spine.

'If he looks at me that way again,' says Ethan sitting up, 'I'll ram his head through the window.' He throws a brace of savage looks across the carriage. His bloodshot eyes roll before he subsides on the seat again.

Kasi replies, in a pleasant-enough tone, beating his oddly sensuous, long eyelashes. 'Not before you tell him. Then, we'll put him through the glass.'

You feel an urgent need to get away from both of them but, simultaneously, you want to manoeuvre yourself between them and the angel on the floor. You can't sit and watch someone beat up a prepubescent kid.

Meanwhile, the beautiful boy refuses to lift his concentration from the patterns on the floor but his tears have stopped. Two wise but ineffectual moves.

You place your hands on your book and lean forward. You intend asking Kasi questions about the suburbs through which you're passing, establishing yourself in a light and animated tone as a harmless tourist. Which you are.

He grunts and turns to face you.

'Can you tell me about Claremont? From here, I can see a lot of trees. Are there places to moor your boat by the river?' you ask.

'It's a rich suburb,' he says 'Next to Peppermint Grove. Where wankers live, often just the two of them with fourteen bedrooms and ten bathrooms. Stinking rich.'

'Mining money?'

'May...be.'

'What about Swanbourne? Would you like to live there?'

'How do you know I don't?' he replies, dragging his eyes away from the boy on the floor, to glare at you.

'Do you?' You smile, hoping to amend your mistake.

'I probably will one day.'

Station signs flash by. The Manga man alights at Cottesloe. Kasi begins to confide his back-story or at least one he thinks you will find appealing. He comes from Melbourne, didn't like school, but Perth is okay. He sounds articulate. You decide he has a mother and a father who at some point showed an interest in him. You keep trying verbally to hold him at bay. Ask him questions that lead away from the school's failure to keep him. What does he like doing best? Does he like music?

You get nothing back. He shrugs. Then recommends that you go to the Maritime Museum at Freo for the shipwrecks, and to be sure and eat at Fisherman's Wharf.

You nod and while you think of more questions, you point out the unsettling sight of a black hawk, buffeted by wind, flying backwards past the train window.

He barely turns his head. Suddenly, apropos of nothing, he stands up—how can this happen while conversing with someone once adept at social discourse?—*and* with no further warning but a reflex fondling of his balls, launches himself across the carriage.

Your heart lurches.

The beautiful boy looks up from examining the minute striations on the palms of his hands: life lines, ancient scars. You think, after all, he can't be more than twelve.

But his potential aggressor has your full attention. His hair is unfashionably spiked and glitters with some kind of stale fruity gel that you smell as he passes. He wants you to watch. Perhaps to intervene and stop him. You, rupturing his performance will delight him. It will cause a scene. He will draw out the moment before he acts. You know this and you will *not* rattle his cage.

Kasi drops on his haunches to whisper into the boy's ear. Through his spiky hair you notice scars like evidence of lightning strikes on the back of his scalp. Hairdressers should be compelled to notify authorities. The boy turns his head to the window, doesn't speak. His skin shines with perspiration. The older boy weighs up his seeming passivity. Perhaps he is warning the kid to keep away from his friend Ethan—knows his work—wants to save him from chemical violence.

You glance uneasily around the carriage. You think of the shape of a body in a shattered window, on a train travelling at speed. The damage to the boy's beautiful skin when flung by angry young gods.

Kasi retreats to his seat and begins flexing his skinny arms. They look quite white in the sunlight, with their smattering of black moles.

You resume your burble with less confidence. He pretends an avuncular politeness beyond his years—the little shit has made his point and you should treat him with respect—relaxed, leaning back in his seat, left ankle crossed across his right knee. So erratic. Earlier, you could not help but like the positive aspects of his personality. His intelligence. His certain acceptance that an educated fellow-commuter will play this game with him. Could he mean well, after all? Your ignorance about Perth pleases him, you know this, as he points out landmarks, tells you he will help you find the Fremantle Arts Centre, once the Claremont Mental Hospital, when you arrive.

Intermittently the boy on the floor lifts his head and sniffs the air around him like quarry or like someone selling something. The train carriage has lost any hope of being a neutral space. In either case, who among the passengers, deep in books, tapping on keyboards, chatting on their phones, massaging leather bags, will defend him? None, you surmise and he knows it although people often surprise you in crises. What looks like suturing thread but is probably acrylic cotton holds parts of his worn, green coat together. In his disguised agitation he has snapped a section apart revealing only the golden curves of his immature chest. He tugs the lapels together and attempts the difficult feat of disappearing into the floor.

*Get off at the next stop,* you send by telekinesis. *Don't stand up until the last possible moment. Then run.*

✦

The train brakes at Mosman and a grey-skirted schoolgirl jumps on, taking the seat beside you. Instead of wearing her ribboned straw hat she holds it against her blue blazer; no doubt a hangable offence. You *will* her to be quiet.

Kasi appears immediately drawn to her and deftly restarts your conversation in an effort to show his best side. Now that is charitable.

An ostensibly respectable adult talking to the boy upsets the girl's radar and she gives him eye contact. She should not. She should keep her head down.

He becomes excited again, leaning forward from his bench seat, baring his rickety teeth in our general direction. You imagine his mind discarding and ticking points that he thinks will interest the schoolgirl. Nothing too personal. He tells you again which road you should take when you disembark at Freo. He asks *her* if she likes to study.

The schoolgirl has scraped her hair back from her forehead and pinned service badges on her lapels; she is an advertisement for the values education offered at her expensive school. She wants to help and she begins to chip in on your tourist conversation with the boy. You are gracious and try to steer the conversation away from him but it is too late.

Her voice is sweet, refined and pleasant. Friendly.

He is not unattractive with his wide crooked smile, his eagerness to engage. But unpredictable.

He speaks more slowly. Moves smoothly into an anecdote about his stay in a Melbourne hospital. There was nothing physically wrong with him, he says. They'd locked him up and pumped him full of drugs for nothing. He'd had to do a heap of tests. More details slide into place. Although he doesn't say so, it is clear he has been detained for three weeks by mental health provisions.

The schoolgirl seems curiously unaware of his sense of thwarted entitlement, or is scrupulously polite. 'I quite like tests,' the girl says. Perhaps she acts deliberately obtuse. Is she passive aggressive?

Momentarily, he switches his attention back to the boy on the floor, who places his head in his hands. Kasi reminds you of your dog, toying with two mice…letting one limp away a certain distance but keeping an eye on it as he bats the second one with his paw.

'Well done,' he says, his attention returning to the schoolgirl. 'To do so well at exams. I hope you like university. Not for me. I couldn't concentrate at school. I was smart and everything but…'

You turn your head away to the window. You want to take the girl's hand and apologise. *Don't talk to him. Really. I misled you.*

To your great relief, the girl rises and reaches for the strap, leaving you to focus on the cherub-faced boy on the floor. He is dragging small change from his jacket pocket, cupping his hand to count the coins, perhaps to see if he has a sufficient number to buy food or a bottle of water.

Kasi and the schoolgirl continue chatting until the next stop where she gets off.

He stares at her legs as she alights. 'Nice girl.' He waves to her. 'I can take you to the Maritime Museum if you want,' he says inviting you back into the conversation.

'Oh, thank you,' you say.

He points it out in the distance, layered wings of silvery-white on the point, rather like the Sydney Opera House.

'I should find both places, I think.' How will you shake him off? 'Perhaps you could give me directions.'

'Really nice girl.'

'Sweet.'

'She was a bit suspicious of me,' he adds.

'I don't think so.'

'Yes, she was.'

'Well, you can't blame her in a way.'

He prickles up.

You lost his trust.

'Do you mean my tattoo? '

You shake your head. It is small, as far as tattoos go; you hadn't noticed it on his scrawny shoulder.

He clenches his fists. 'What do you mean?'

'Well, some boys don't have a good track-record with girls. Not everyone is kind and polite like you.'

'Yeah. That's right.'

'She has to keep herself safe,' you say.

He nods. His friend sprawls looking half-alive, throws out a fruity cough that makes him nurse his chest with one hand.

You look away, scan the carriage for fascinating details. The boy on the floor remains motionless. Perhaps he is frozen, in terror. Resignation.

Before the last stop you try to ease out of the conversation, watch the beautiful boy stand up and move to the middle door to exit at Fremantle. Two passengers queue behind him, preparing to alight. When the train screeches to a stop Kasimir and Ethan swing out of their seats and into the aisle—in no great hurry but close enough to reach around and touch him—once more gripping their damp, scrunched tee shirts against their crotches, as they shoulder their way up behind him. Ethan sniffs and coughs into his tee shirt. You stand, fingers searching your tote bag for your phone. Who should you call? The postdoc? He shouldn't be far away? A transit guard? Haven't seen one. One hand on the strap you edge forward.

They swing away on the balls of their feet following the boy, who has his head down trying to weave around disembarking passengers as he trudges forward through the railway turnstile. He hides behind a curtain of hair that has flopped into his face.

Before they reach the roadside, Kasi lunges forward to hiss something in the boy's ear and takes hold of his arm. And as if to dismiss *you*, he spins around so that you are face to face again and calls out, 'turn right here and follow the next street to the water.'

You nod and thank him. Even from a distance, you hear his mate grumbling, only compos enough to fling hostile looks about him.

The first blow falls. In your struggle to reach the boy you drop Greer's book. 'Stop it,' you cry. 'He's my nephew.' You call on your inchoate friendship. 'Please. Kasi…mir.'

He releases him, punishing his arm with one last thump, and turns towards you as if you've betrayed him. 'Why didn't you say so, you dumb bitch?'

His friend shambles forward, stepping over a bedraggled black bird facedown in the gutter, a stream of blood trickling from beneath its beak. Poor kite.

You seize your newly adopted nephew, slinging your arm around his slight shoulders. He tries to shrug you off. You decide to reschedule your date with the young academic until you've clarified your thinking about Rembrandt's transmogrification of Michelangelo's famous drawing of a beautiful boy. You tug the boy through the graceful 100 year old station archway, into the twenty-first century, towards the esplanade and a feed of fish and chips. Glancing back, you see them, Kasimir and Ethan, giving you the finger before turning in the opposite direction.

---

**Gay Lynch** teaches creative writing and English at Flinders University. She has published *Apocryphal and Literary Influences on Galway Diasporic History* (2010), *Cleanskin* (2006), an adult psycho-fem-thriller, short stories, educational children's texts and academic papers, and is presently working on a resubmit of her historical novel to a publisher. Most recently, she published 'Pumped' in *Sleepers Almanac:* No 8 (2013).

# A Real Looker

## Jo Lennan

Once, at my father's place for a week in the holidays, I spent several nights on a boat called the *Marilyn.* A fixer-upper yacht, it had its own jetty at the end of Alby's land, where the patchy grass gave way to mangroves and mud flats. I was old enough, at thirteen, to know why I slept on board instead of in the house, and still young enough to love the novelty anyway. I loved eating on deck; Alby would bring me down a plate. I loved the nightly shimmy into my berth and sleeping bag, and lying awake to hear the lapping of the upper Hawkesbury River.

Alby was new to me that year, almost as novel as the yacht. He had until recently existed as a face in photographs and an annual scrawl in a Hallmark card. Then he had telephoned my mother, asking to have contact. Our first meeting had been at the Sizzler in West Gosford, our second at a truck stop where, from a framed poster, Marilyn Monroe laughed and posed over a subway grate. On these occasions I met a man with a thick unruly beard that captured crumbs and sauce globules. He was a person of quick affections and unclear occupation—although not quite a mechanic, he was brilliant with engines and effortlessly fixed our ailing Datsun 200B. With Mum he was flirtatious; she called him an old charmer. What followed was a flurry of long-distance calls—a courtship not of romance but of filial connection. We were trying out the idea of being a family, if a poorer sort than the regular live-in version. Alby had one of those already, made up of his wife Gail and Dan, their grown-up son, but he told us Gail was coming round to the idea of a visit. There was talk of the holidays, then the excitement of laying plans. I imagined a living room like out of the Bradys, with a staircase to hang over and someone cooking in the kitchen.

Gail, as it turned out, was small of build, wore cargo pants and, when I arrived, came out of a house that only had one level. She was business-like and cool but made me a welcome cup of tea, bringing it to the patio table with a plate of gingernuts. Dan, my half-brother, emerged from a workshed. Dark and bare-chested, with his shirt tied around his head, he looked like my idea of an Afghan soldier. 'What, cat got your tongue?' he said as he grabbed two biscuits before disappearing back to the sheds.

The house was to be off limits; this was made clear early on. But the yacht was my domain. And the *Marilyn,* said Alby, was a beauty, a real looker. She called to the hearts of wild, romantic men. As someone who liked to tinker as much as he liked to sail, my father had felt compelled to buy and fix the vessel, restoring her gradually to the height of glamour. For the first days of my stay this was all we did—scouring and sanding and oiling the wood trim. I was glad to be enlisted, glad to work alongside my dad, glad to see my tan deepen to match his. But come day three or four—for they had begun to run together—there was an unexpected tools-down announcement.

'Jenny love,' he said, grinning his rogue's grin. 'We're going to a meeting.' What this meeting was, or where, he wouldn't yet divulge, keeping the secret close to his chest like a winning hand of cards. He had me finish up on the section I'd been oiling—'We can't leave my girl in a state of neglect'—and knelt to seal the varnish tins and padlock the hatch.

It was mid-morning and bright. The sun inched up the she-oaks. Passing the house, I saw a face at the kitchen window. It was Gail with her cat's bum mouth, pursing, disapproving. Well, I thought with triumph, I'm *here*. I was invited. I went on up the hill, swinging my arms freely. I was there, like it or not. Alby's daughter in the flesh.

'Oi!' called a voice when I stepped into the sheds. These were dim and filled with junk—automobile parts, a bunch of upturned shopping trolleys and a decrepit LandCruiser raised up on brick blocks. Underneath this vehicle protruded a pair of legs. The legs belonged to Dan, who was wriggling out and saying, 'The sheds are out of bounds, girls have to get out.' He was grinning as he said this, and his grin was just like Alby's. He was flirting, as I was, with what it meant to have a sibling.

'*You* get out,' I said. 'I'm going with Dad.'

My use of 'Dad' was a kind of dare and Dan gazed back, eyes narrowed. 'Going with Dad where?'

'To a very important meeting.' This was Alby, coming in. He was carrying a crate. 'Got the prototype,' he said, heading for the van. And Dan the smart-aleck, who had nothing to say now, flicked my legs with a length of cord as he slid beneath the troopie.

The drive took us around the bends of Mangrove Mountain. Alby sped with glee, saying, 'Cops keep to the highway.' We had the windows down and the radio up loud, tuned to a station playing '70s rock anthems. Raising his voice above the music, Alby spoke about his meeting. He was going to present an invention he hoped to sell, a device for steadying the steering of a swivel wheel. 'Shopping trolleys,' he said. 'Everything with a swivel wheel, right up to fighter jets.'

'Wow,' I said, impressed.

'First of all, it's trolleys. Think about it, love. How happy would you be if you could steer the things straight? To the supermarket moguls, that's worth a lot.'

'Are they who you're seeing then, the moguls?'

'Yeah. We are taking it to moguls.'

We came to a shopping centre on the outskirts of Gosford. It sat there, flat and white, marooned in a tarmac sea. Getting out with his crate, Alby told me to wait an hour. I sunned my shins on the dashboard and played the radio. I wasn't sure how long it was but then Alby was back again, flashing a wide smile as he yanked the driver's door.

'What did I tell you, Jen?'

'They wanted to buy it?'

'They've made us a starting offer.'

I clapped my hands. It was the way Alby said 'us', gathering me into his good fortune—this was what was stunning, what filled me with a sense of promise.

Going back it was all downhill. On hitting the longer stretches, Alby gave a happy shout and turned off the engine to save on gas. Whenever he did this trick, the radio cut out too, so all you heard as you sailed down was the clattering of parrots then that thrilling tear of air before the combustion kicked.

✦

That night, lying in bed, I heard voices from the house. They travelled down the hill and across the darkened water. It was Alby and his wife, arguing about something. I couldn't pick out their actual words but knew it had to do with me. In the morning, Alby came to shepherd me to the van. 'No, love,' he assured me. 'You don't have to go home yet.'

We drove toward Sydney—the northwest suburbs of the city. He took me to my cousins' place, a beige two-storey house, and dropped me in the driveway. 'Just to give Gail a break,' he said, looking embarrassed. When my aunt came out of the door, his discomfort increased. Plastering on a grin, he greeted my mother's no-nonsense older sister. 'Sharon, long time no see.'

'Yes,' she said drily. 'Thirteen years, Albert.'

At which Alby, still grinning, said he'd best push off.

My cousins, Sue and Lori, tried to cheer me up. They were twins, in their late teens, both going to uni. To me they appeared impossibly worldly people, sophisticated in the ways of men and public transport. Taking the train to Town Hall Station, we went to Grace Brothers with its gleaming makeup counters. There my cousins took turns dabbing things on my face. 'So pretty,' they sighed, and yet when I bought a blue eye shadow they only disapproved, saying I should have bought the powder instead of the cream version, which apparently was given to sliding off your lids. 'You'll learn,' Lori said, handing back the offending pot.

In the evening I spoke to Mum on Aunt Sharon's cordless phone. Mum knew all about the blow-up between Alby and Gail; he had called her to organise the last-minute Sydney trip. 'He said he's sorry, hon. Says a day or two more will do it.' Alby had also told her of his windfall deal. 'Just think of it,' she said. 'What we'll be able to do. We'll get new tyres for the car. Or buy a new car altogether.' She spoke of a holiday to see the Great Barrier Reef, of buying clothes for me and a treadmill for herself. We talked like this a while so that when I got off the call, handing the phone on to my aunt, I felt new seeds of hope sprouting in my chest. I went through to watch TV, but when the next commercial came I was shocked to see my aunt was crying. Hiccupping and red-eyed, she stood at the rangehood. Lori, seeing what I saw, shut the concertina doors, screening off the kitchen where her mother wept.

'What's happened?' I asked.

Lori's answer was as cryptic as one of her uni readers, the heavy photocopied tomes she would pore over, pen in hand. 'Mum sometimes gets frustrated. She made choices, too, you know. She found a man she thought was able to support her.'

I thought about Uncle Ben, who had a bulbous nose. He had never struck me as frustrating. He was kind-hearted and calm and walked softly in loafers. Unable to make out the cause of the upset, I let the matter slide and picked the ends of my fingernails. I had other things on my mind, such as why weren't my cousins happy that I was coming into money? They'll see, I thought, and I pictured them, weeks on, seeing Alby's invention on the evening news. I imagined the story angle—local man makes good, grocery shopping set to get easier, etcetera. That night and coming nights I slept in a bed that did not rock, missing first the yacht and then my own bedroom in the house my mother rented from the Housing Department.

In the end it was not two nights but four at my cousins' house—the rest of the week I was meant to stay at Alby's. When he came to pick me up, we headed straight on up the highway, passing the turnoff that led to his place on the Hawkesbury. We drove northwards for four hours to the rendezvous with Mum. This was in another town, on another great slow river. When we pulled off for the park beside the iron bridge, I saw her Datsun there already, parked and waiting for us. Mum was standing in the shade, large and luminous, a perspiring white-skinned figure in a loose sundress. When I got out she hugged me tightly and made cooing pigeon sounds. Putting her chin over my shoulder, she said hello to Alby. 'So what was the counter-offer?' she asked him playfully. 'Wait, I can guess—'

'Can you?' he said, grinning. Turning, he was grabbing bags out of the van—all my bags and books and pillows—to stow them in the Datsun.

'Alby?' Mum said, letting go of me. 'Has the company called you back?'

He laughed. 'It must've knocked their socks off when I turned them down. Don't worry. They'll come back. This is about—' He stressed his words. '—a smooth consumer experience.'

'They haven't called.'

I spoke up. 'They will. They will call, won't they, Dad?'

'Sure they're going to call.'

Mum was looking at Alby, her lover of long ago. For years she had seen his absence as something almost cosmic—a fact beyond her control or his or that of any mortal being—but now anger registered in her pale face. In watching her I knew that there would be no windfall, no cheque to be written out for a Monopoly amount. I grasped this even as my father kept on talking about corporate strategies. But I could not have guessed what my mother would do next, which was to suddenly launch forward in all her alabaster bulk and land a kiss on Alby's beard. 'Oh, I'm sure you're right!' Her laugh was high, coquettish.

Alby briefly looked uncertain, then he grabbed her bird-like hand. He planted his own rash kiss on that waxy skin. My mother laughed again, more deeply this time, with her head thrown back like Marilyn Monroe. As I watched she grew radiant, and I saw for the first time how she resembled the actress—or resembled the woman Monroe might have become if she had lived to put on weight and take solace in cask wine.

Standing there like that, with their backs against the river, my parents looked as untroubled as they did in the old photo that sat on Mum's bedroom dresser. They were their younger sailing selves, smiling into a fair wind. It was I who was troubled, seeing something pass between them, something I would later wish I had never seen. It was no ordinary display between two grown-up people, troubling as that might be for a teenager. What I glimpsed instead was their love as it had been, a joyous terrifying force. It transported the two of them to somewhere else entirely, an all-consuming place where no one else could live or breathe. I turned away, unnerved. Years on, I would oscillate, blaming first one then the other, and then pitying them both and finally myself, because who of us wants to know about passion like that?

'Alby,' Mum said. 'Goodness. Your daughter is watching.'

She took her hand away, a favour withdrawn. We got into the Datsun and started the long drive home. Alby went home too—home to his other, actual family, to his worksheds and his yacht.

After that, he telephoned, although less often than before. He reported his progress on the boat. The mast was going in at last and the second-hand stereo. The Dacron main had been selected (hand-sewn boltropes, hand-sewn rings). Full of talk of the maiden voyage, he said, 'You'd better be ready, Jen.' And I felt a rush of pleasure as I pictured it, the day when the new-look beauty would cruise down the wide river, do a little pirouette out front of the marina, and put in long enough to be loved by all.

---

**Jo Lennan** was born on New South Wales' south coast, and studied in Sydney, Adelaide and Oxford. Her writing appears in *The Monthly*, *Meanjin*, *The Economist*, *Intelligent Life* and *Time*, and has also been included in Black Inc's *Best Australian Essays*. Jo is currently working on a novel, which won a Varuna HarperCollins Manuscript Award in 2013.

# Athina and the Sixty-Nine Calorie Burn

Rosemary Jackson

## #1

I just feel sooo ugly sometimes. Just letting you know. All of you out there, like me, trying to Take Some Control.

OMFG! I AM UP TO FIFTY-FOUR! FIFTY-FOUR FUCKING KILOS!!!!

I seriously hate myself. I do! Before I know, I'll be as fat as that bitch Loretta McArdle! Lol!

Anyway…most of you don't know her. And she doesn't even realise that she is fat. Or doesn't care. Which is disgraceful! She's almost definitely a Lesbian!!

I've started this blog cos I want to be a writer.

SO ALL YOU WRITERS OUT THERE. Join Me!

But Most Importantly, I'm going on a Weight Loss Journey and I realise that these things are easier when you share them with friends. And maybe there'll be heaps of you out there who know what it's like to not be skinny and have your Mum tell you that she loves you just the way you are and when you see your Dad, to have him say that his girlfriend Carly's probably about the same size as you and She's beautiful, but You know that she's at least a size fourteen!!!

So that's a bit about me. And BTW…my name is Charlotte!

I think it's really important to Share stuff about yourself because then you discover heaps about how you think when you didn't even know you thought like that. Or other people thought like that. If you get what I mean.

I've found this really cool website for pro-ana's. Which is what I've decided I am. They've got pretend names and stuff because if you're seriously pro-ana your parents and teachers start giving you shit. There's lots of cool ideas for fooling people like having bits of carrot and celery and shit and kind of nibbling them all day so people think you're eating all the time BUT there's hardly any calories and then people stop hassling you.

Because we Gotta Stay Strong! And these chicks are all really supportive of each other, so that's what we're gonna do here. MWAAH!

Here are some Positives!!

**THINGS I LIKE ABOUT MYSELF**

1. I don't care about what other people say about me. I'm just myself!
2. I've got good skin.
3. I'm a pretty happy-go-lucky chick. I don't get stressed about shit.
4. I've got big eyes. (Even though they're brown, not blue!)
5. I've found a way to curl my hair so it looks Natural.
6. I'm adventurous about Sex (def not a Slut!) and I'm open to the universe. Because it's all about the adventure!!!

So what's on your list? I discovered that there's things I'm really proud of. You can probably think of heaps more! Go Girlfriend!!

## #2

OK. So I found a way to deal with food!!!! It's really working!!!

I was at Dad's place this week, where it's easier to miss meals as Carly and Dad both hate cooking and don't stress about whether you eat at regular times, so I don't need to do breakfast. But then it's harder in another way because they get lots of take-away and I just looove KFC. And of course if you get a meal deal you get chips and Coke. I always choose the Zero though, as there's absolutely no calories. And sometimes they include a salad. Which is Healthy!!!

BUT Anyway, I was going to tell you about this way I found of Dealing with Food! It's my eighteenth birthday in eight weeks and I want to have lost at least eight kilos by then.

So FYI…

SET FOOD RULES. Pick the ones that you can keep and stick to them. Religiously, like to Buddha or Ganesh or something, except they're Yours!

GRADUALLY ADD MORE RULES. When you've kept them, add another, like if you like potatoes and you've stopped eating them, see what other white foods you can stop too!

REWARD YOURSELF. You've been so good, give yourself

a treat, but not food, maybe download extra iTunes or whatever puts you in a HAPPY place.

FIND A PICTURE OF SOMETHING THAT MAKES YOU FEEL SICK. Seems crazy but you get this picture and stick it next to you while you're eating. After a few meals, keep changing the picture to other things that're really unpleasant. Just days later you realise this kind of psychology is working and you are now associating Any Eating with Bad Karma!!!

I believe that when you take charge of your body the universe starts working for you.     It's happening for me!!!

✦

He towels himself down. The tremors are there, but they're slight today. Fifty solid minutes. Not bad. Not bad for an old cunt. Geez it was freezing in there. Bit of a breeze, a few clouds, but the sun is steady enough. So what's with the tremors? Even though he's wearing this new wetsuit. The 350 Vanquish. Cost an arm and a leg. Looks fucking beautiful, good flexibility, but now he's cold.

The shivers come from beneath his collarbones, tauten his neck and contract his jaws. He shakes his head, spinning the droplets into the air. Then he releases his shoulder blades and stands, legs apart and breathes out facing the sea, rock solid. One swift breath out, then slow and steady does it, he draws air into his lungs, One-Two-Three-Four- Five-Hold. Exhale. After ten repetitions he stops. His head feels light and spacious. The tremors are gone. A soft grunt signifies his satisfaction. Things are as they ought to be. He picks up his towel and slips his feet into his thongs.

A gaggle of young women pass him. He sniffs the air. No

one in that lot that needs to be fucked down to a size twelve. They're all little birdlike creatures, fine collarbones gleaming through pale brown, impossibly soft skin, and small neat breasts that sit high on their chests. Flat stomachs. And the legs. Smooth calf muscles, thighs shaped like saplings. All have pretty faces. How can they not have? They're young. Takes a few years before the creases and rolls of dissatisfaction show themselves. Two are blondes, one's hair is seal black and the fourth has fat auburn curls. He's not a narrow-minded man in shedding his favours. He prides himself on that. Any hair colour will do.

The auburn curly-haired girl looks his way. Her eyes had taken him in before as he'd peeled off his wetsuit. Let her look. He's in pretty good shape. Flat torso, muscular shoulders and strong legs. His face is the dead spit of his old man's at this age, but that never stopped his dad from pulling the women. And his equipment never lets him down. She looks him straight in the face and grins. She has good teeth, probably courtesy of some North Adelaide dentist, and fine lips with a hint of pale pink lipstick on them, that colour that only young girls can get away with that makes him want to place his lips on hers and cradle her curls in his hand. Fucking beautiful. And fresh. Like the first cold beer on a hot day. Like that gulp of air when you surface and you've been underwater too long.

'I'm here every day at the same time.'

'Are you talking to me?'

'You know I am.'

'I might not be here then.'

'See you tomorrow.'

'Why would I be back?'

'You look like the sort of girl that can go off on her own. Have a bit of an adventure.'

**#3**

I'm about to start on a new phase of my life. I'm not about to let my old patterns of negativity and self-doubt rule my life. I'm in charge of me!!

I was with my girlfriends at the beach and I was really proud of myself cos they had all just eaten Macca's and I'd only had two of Jacinta's fries. I was saying to myself 'Food never tastes as good as thin feels' and totally getting into the vibe of that, when I saw him. From behind. OMG!! I totally knew that something was going to happen. He stood looking toward the sea like he was in charge of it, like it belonged to him. And when he turned around he looked straight at me! He has these piercing eyes, and their blueness felt like hot ice. And I felt like he knew me.

**#4**

FYI his name is Rob, he's the lead singer in an Indie band and he's completely different from any other man I've ever known! He's experienced so much of life, and even though he's older than me, well a lot older actually, I feel that I've finally found someone that I can really connect with, on lots of different levels...

One of the most important things for us to realise is that there Are men who get the fact that we're pro-ana and are Really into it and think that we're Hot.

Also...I'm just gonna say it...SEX BURNS CALORIES!!!

Google it if you don't believe me! Men burn more than chicks, but we still burn. At least sixty-nine! Kissing's extra. And heaps more if you moan and make lots of noise!

(Advantage of being with a man rather than a boy is that you can moan like crazy cos he's got his own place) Bahahahaha!

Reckon I burned at least three hundred calories last night!!

✦

Every time it hits him. The petal soft skin. The angular hip bones jutting out below the delicate curves of the stomach. Little hard brown nipples on tiny breasts that he will engulf with his mouth, nipping and sucking. The surprising tensile strength of the cunt, drawing him in to its molten depths. He gets lost. For a time. Swept off into a warm protective wave of what, for lack of a better word, he calls love. He feels invaded by it and feels his carapace slough off, as if to make room for the raw flesh underneath. He always loses his shell.

He gives the process great care. He is meticulous. Like a good song, you play it fresh every time, you give it what it needs. In your hands it turns into something miraculous. Charlotte, that's her name. Charlotte, is so young that she has no idea of the miracle of youth and all that it uncovers in him. Tasting her, he wants to drink her all up. As she comes, her high voice sings in exultation of her own power and his adoration of her. She repeats his name. Over and over. This normally unsettles him. He usually stops that caper. But right now, it's as if he's never heard it before. Who he is. What he can be. Warrior, Protector, Father, Lover.

This Charlotte's got stamina. He'll say that for her. And she's a damn good liar. Eleven at night, resting in between bouts, her phone rings. She grins, and as she speaks, her voice takes the persuasive tones of the good child, reassuring her mother. Yes, she was having a sleepover at Jacinta's. Yes, they were tucking into lasagne and chips as they spoke. After, she races into the bathroom. Squeals of 'Oh my God, Oh my fucking God! I've lost another two kilos!' She leaps on him like a kitten, all nips and licks and mews, squirming against him in delight. He rolls her over, pins her against the bed, and with hard strokes, settles her down.

Later, she shows him her favourite websites on her phone. She reveals what she calls her 'pro-ana' name. Athina. A-Thin-a Beauty. Does he get it? Her eyes are like chocolate pools; auburn hair tumbles over her face, lapping at her nipples. He gets it.

He likes to cook for her. He's a fucking great cook. Tiny morsels of food are all she will eat. He serves it to her in bed on a black lacquer tray, off fine bone china, with silver utensils and a diamond cut crystal glass of Perrier water with a sliver of lemon. He feeds her and as she opens her mouth to him, he places the food on her warm pink tongue. Sometimes she calls him Daddy.

## #5

Hello again. It's been soo long since I've written, nearly three weeks, and I'm living the life I've always wanted. It's about three words.

I'M IN CHARGE.

- I'm up to fifty crunches and forty-five pushups a day. I jog for at least fifty minutes before school (leaving early in my uniform so mum doesn't know what I'm doing) and same again after school b4 mum gets home
- I don't eat lunch at school, so it saves money. REWARD! I bought myself a new gym top! YAY
- I've convinced Mum to let me go to Yoga on Wednesdays and sleepover at Jacinta's (Rob's!!) Then it's Dad's place from Friday night to Sunday night. I'm Taking the Freedom I Choose!

Haven't had a period in a while and went crazy thinking I

was pregnant. But Rob's had a vasectomy. He's so sweeeet! Imagine being Fat for Nine Months. Gross…He loves me skinny. Most Importantly, So Do I!!!

School's kind of boring. 'That's not News to Me!' I hear you say…Bahahaha Seriously tho, I was one of those girls that teachers always said was 'promising'. I still love Dance. Ms Thompson, the dance teacher, told me I was looking really fabulous since I'd lost the weight. So it proves that discerning people notice when you work on yourself!

✦

For her eighteenth birthday he buys her a pink, pure silk slip and G-string. Strictly legal now. The slip is as pure as her skin. He dresses her in it, then thumbing the G-string aside he fucks her with care. As she removes the G-string for the next round she shrieks.

'JEESUS!'

'What?'

'These are size ten! You bought me a size ten! How fucking fat do you think I am?'

Her face is as crumpled as the pink slip. But a different shade of pink. An ugly shade. There is spittle on her lips.

'I thought you GOT me! I thought you knew my body! I'm an eight! Jesus!!'

She pulls away from him, curling up, foetal.

Fucking hell. The pain in his left calf cramps down to his heel. The toes curl up. He breathes and flexes. She is still sobbing. He pulls her toward him and rocks. She slows her sobs to a whimper. He breathes again as he feels the cramp lessening. And senses the new skin on himself growing, thickening.

She sleeps.

**#6**

You know, having a relationship takes a lot of work!! Just because you know you're destined for each other doesn't mean that there's not heaps of misunderstanding along the way.

No One Else should have the Power to Control the Way You See Yourself!!

If they can't see you as you want to be seen...Whatever it takes hey girlfriend?

Here's another (2) thinspirational sayings:

**Do it for the body you have always wanted** cos **You have nothing to lose except all this Fat.**

I used to wonder what it felt like having 'thighs that don't touch'.

Now I know!!

One of the things that can happen when you're working this hard on yourself is that you get a bit dizzy. It's normal. Don't Let it Put you Off! You just need to rest a little (not too much) then you'll be fine!

✦

There's almost a routine now. Charlotte arrives in her school uniform, he divests her of most of it, and they fuck. In the hallway, or on the stairs and sometimes, on the bare wooden floors of the studio amongst the detritus of cords and amps. He carries her up to the bedroom. Then he feeds her and they fuck again.

This time she comes in her gym clothes, carrying her enormous school backpack. She is sweating.

'I ran all the way. Six point three kilometres! That's four hundred and ten calories burned!'

He admires her pluck, the fine sheen of sweat on her skin. He'd like to lick it off her. All of her.

'No don't touch me. I'm gross. Let me have a shower first!'

She brushes past him, up the stairs, into the bathroom. He shrugs, collects the tray and takes it up to the bedroom. He has a treat. A dozen Sydney rock oysters to share and the finest tender shavings of smoked salmon. Forty minutes pass. She emerges, a towel on her head and a scowl on her face.

'And don't think you can keep feeding me like this! Everyone knows oysters are full of cholesterol! That's why I keep having so much sex with you. I need to work it off!'

He picks up the oysters. One by one he pours them down his throat. He takes a sip of water. Then, with the hard silver fork, he places the salmon into his mouth, until the plate is gleaming and empty. He finishes the water.

He fits comfortably into his new shell. That was a fucking beautiful meal.

His blue eyes look bang into hers.

'Time for you to go I think.'

## #7

Love can be so cruel.  I can't think, can't do my schoolwork…And I def can't eat. I've told Mum I'm really sick. She's heaps worried about me.

I Just Want to Die!!!

The thing is, you find someone you Think accepts you the way you are. Someone who Tells you all the time that You're Beautiful!!

Someone who is supportive of you achieving your goals in life. Encouraging your full potential.

I was getting SICK of SEX all the time anyway…

I've learned one BIG IMPORTANT LESSON!!

You can't trust anyone. That Someone who accepts you and supports you and thinks you are Beautiful as your thin lovely self, that Someone is You!

So here's a saying that I've created. Out of my own pain and struggle.
It comes to You from Me, Athina Beauty. Mwamwamwa.

**Thin is Pure Beauty, so Starving is Our Duty!**

---

**Rosemary Jackson** enjoys telling stories. She has worked as a teacher, an actor for a performing troupe in schools and as a role-player for both corporate and medical education. She is a graduate of the Masters of Creative Writing programme at the University of Adelaide.

# Walking with Alice

Kimberley Zeneth

Late afternoon Alice drags me out the back door.
*Come on! Pick flowers with me!*

She knows how to lift the pole up the length of one arm and pull the gate towards her with the other. She slips purposefully through as it swings. The hollow metal clangs shut behind her. I follow. Another clang.

We tug, pull violently at and sever the necks of flowers all the way up the driveway.
Her little white hands grip. Her strong skinny arms tremble. She pulls with force and she grits her teeth as she concentrates. We garner flowers of so many suburban sorts. First she picks bougainvillea, huge clumps of tangerine and hot pink stripped of their stems by her eager insistence, then skinny white geraniums and a wilting rose.

She's pulling at more plump sprigs of bougainvillea. She has trouble with those.
*Look. Yank it sideways, at the bottom of the stem. See? Before the thorns start.* It's a skill quickly learnt and she demonstrates her ability all the way along the fence line, leaning at forty degrees, holding her breath, making the little sounds of effort.

We pick our fill of flowers. It takes us a gentle age to reach the end of the driveway.

Our hands are full, the stems mostly too short to hold in a posy. She clutches them in a loose fist. Colours poke through the bars of her fingers. We walk barefoot, her nude, me in my frilly orange bikini nearly dry from swimming in the sea two hours ago. Our hands spill the confetti of lost petals as we stride the last stretch of driveway to the grass. I listen, already wistful, to the scuffs of our feet on the old concrete.

*Sit here with me,* she says. I thud my thirty-something legs heavily to the ground.

*The grass is itching me* she says standing up, scratching at her legs. I pat my lap, as if she were a cat and she reverses in and sits her little white bottom into my lap. With her head tilted slightly to one side she arranges the flowers on the grass in front of us. I almost stop breathing. She clutches the flowers to her tummy and shoots a cheeky grin up at me. I stare off into the distance to where the deep sea holds whales and manta rays and sharks and sea dragons and whiting and crabs. We rest for a time, lulling ourselves in the warm air.

She plays with a stick, poking it into the dirt. I rub a smudge of dirt from her knee. The skin is a tiny bit rough. I blink down, notice her limbs have grown long. The tops of her feet no longer have that soft chubby bulge. She is a girl child, not a baby anymore.

Alice jumps up. *We could pick those flowers!* She points across the road to a vacant block where wild daisies bob in a thin sea breeze that is lifting us. She stands up still clutching hands full of bougainvillea. *We can leave those ones here,* I say. She lays them out on the grass, arranges them solemnly. Then we walk over, her catching my hand to cross the road. We tip toe gingerly on the coarse bitumen road. It looks freshly laid.

More like a field than a block, the land has a stand of trees and rabbit holes and large rocks. She squats to look at the ants. We crouch, focus and stare. Hundreds of tiny ants march along the edge of the field, into and out of a deep hole near the kerb.

*They've made a highway* I say.
*Where are they going?*
*Looking for food. I don't know where. Let's follow them and find out.*
*Can we follow them all the way?* she asks.
I smile.
*Yes. Let's.*

We stand and walk. She keeps her eyes on the trail of ants. It's wider now, a busy freeway seen from an aeroplane.

Her mother, my sister, yells *Put t-shirts on to keep warm.* She brings them out to us.

We walk slowly round the block following the line of ants, their highway uninterrupted by buildings, cars or driveways, stopping to look closely once in a while. When an ant comes near us to sniff our toes or bite us we shuffle back our feet and squeal.

At the corner of the block thick strands of tar dribble out from the edge of the road. I stand on one. It moves, like warm black plasticine.
*Do this with me Alice.*
The tar bulges and feels funny under our feet. We push our

toes and our fingers into the soft, fat bubbles of tar.

I hear a car motor and tug her onto the itchy grass. She follows, blinking analytically at the car as it passes, then looks down again to continue her research. She wipes a little smear of tar on her white T-shirt with the kitten on it.

I lean down to stare at a lawn weed at the edge of the concrete. I pick up a small round grass prickle; a brown, flat seed with curly burrs. I picked these out of my socks walking home from school; childhood in a bush town. It's a bindi with tiny barbs spinning out from a spiral centre. I hold the prickle up against the light blue sky. Its outline is a sun drawn in dark lead pencil.

*Prickle sun!* I say.
*Yes,* she says, *It's our prickle sun. Can I have it?* I hand it over.

We wander further round the curve and come to a lilac bottle brush. She marvels at the flowers, mouth open in gentle awe.
*Fairy floss tree,* she says. *Purple one.*
She grabs a big tuft of lilac flowers in her two hands and pulls with all her might.
*It won't come off,* she says.
*You'll have to bend it back and forth to snap it*, I say. *Here, stand close. Try this.*

Alice works hard, collects five sprigs. She stands, clutching them to her chest like a flower girl. There's a gentle, giving look in her eyes as she says, *You can have this one. I'll keep all these ones.*

We wander further round. *Here,* I say, *I want to pick these ones. I love them. I think they're wild daisies.*

I pluck three of the ragged, pretty weed flowers and hold them up to the sky. Alice lifts her chin to stare with me at the shapes they make against the blue. *They're my favourite silhouette,* I say. *Me too,* says Alice holding up her two. The raggedy shape of them trembling in her hand makes me a sad kind of happy. I close my eyes. I know I won't forget those curling petals—how they reach out, held up against the eve sky, dark magenta shapes which drift in the shallows of those dusty pink clouds, or the shape of her little hand, flat white moons of fingernails, clasping the long, thin stems.

Having come full circle, we sit on the grass by the driveway and blink at a sunset sky. The grass is itchy. She pats me and tells me to make a smaller lap for her to sit in.

A large craggy gum tree waves against the furrowed brow of a brown-blue sky. The cooling breath of late dusk moves across the dry skin of our faces.

*Alice?* I say. She looks over at me and there's a moment.
*I will love you 'til I die,* I say. She says nothing for a minute, then
*Will you die?* She asks.
*We all will.*
*Why?*
*Because bodies get worn out. And I think minds and hearts do too…*
*Will you die today?*
*No not today, not tomorrow, but I will die before you...*
*How do you know?*

She's playing with the lilac fairy floss flower, tickling my skin with it until I have to rub the flesh near my knee.
*I don't really. Maybe I won't, but I hope I do… and I'll die loving you.*
She tickles herself with the flower.

*I hope you won't die,* she says, placing the flower on my knee and says,
*I'll love you too,* with a faint smile, looking at me and then at the sky.

---

**Kimberley Zeneth** has published in journals, books, on parking-meters and on skin. Kim co-wrote a libretto and completed a Master of Creative Writing and two fellowships at Varuna. Her words are on stone sculptures in Adelaide. *Awake During Anaesthetic* (poetry) was published in 2009. She lives in the desert with her beautiful wife.

# Acknowledgements

Rebekah Clarkson's 'A Simple Matter of Aesthetics' was published in *Zettel Magazine,* October, 2014.

Melanie Kinsman's 'A Paper Woman' was published in *The Trouble with Flying,* eds Richard Rossiter with Susan Midalia, Margaret River Press, 2014.

Stefan Laszczuk's 'The Window Winder' was published in *The Body,* eds. Henry Ashley-Brown, Chelsea Avard, Amy T. Matthews, Stephanie Thomson, Wakefield Press, 2004.

Bryan Whalen's 'Duck' was published in *Voiceworks Magazine,* July, 2009.

Bryan Whalen's 'Self Portrait with Angel Olsen' was published in *Scum Magazine,* May, 2013.

# Thank you

Firstly, to the writers. It was a rewarding and enlightening task to work with each of the talented writers in this collection and I am grateful for their love of words and stories. I thank each of them for entrusting me with their precious work. Writers make the world a better place, and this book is proof of that.

My sincere thanks and gratitude go to Anna Solding and MidnightSun Publishing for taking on this project with as much passion as I had for it. Anna's support for Australian writers is inspiring and invigorating.

Special thanks are due to Brian Castro for writing a fascinating and eloquent introduction, and for giving ballast to this collection with the sheer weight of his intelligence. I am also grateful to J.M. Coetzee and Cath Kenneally for their generous endorsements.

Thank you to the University of Adelaide for supporting this project financially.

My gratitude also goes to those people who volunteered their time to review and proofread the manuscript: Anna Solding, Kristin Martin, Tom Di Santo and Allan Taylor.

To the super-talented Kim Lock, who patiently and graciously addressed incoherent and erratic cover design briefs; thank you for always bringing cheerful and positive energy to this project and, of course, for the striking cover design.

On a personal note, I would like to thank Ja Pišem. Month after month, year after year, the members of this writing group provide each other with enduring support, companionship and encouragement. Ja Pišem puts oxygen in my lungs and lightness in my heart and makes me keep working and striving.

And finally, thanks to my family for making everything worthwhile.

Lynette Washington

# From the writers of Breaking Beauty ...

Stories are fascinating things: their origins are often mysterious and where they end up can be unrelated to the wisp of awareness that sparked the writer to sit down in the first place. How does an idea—a smoky, nebulous thing—become a tightly packed narrative? We asked the writers of *Breaking Beauty* where their inspiration came from, and this is what they said.

**Gillian Britton**
***'Beautiful Girl'***

'Beautiful Girl' has always been about the fox—I once saw such a doomed mother fox on a night time country road, and while I didn't actually hit it, I knew the car behind would. The poignancy of the creature's groping to pull herself from the road has lived with me, I think all the more because it was obvious that she was feeding a litter. So it had to be a story about motherhood and survival, but it was years in gestation.

**Rebekah Clarkson**
***'A Simple Matter of Aesthetics'***

We had saved for a long time to pay a carpenter to build a piece of furniture in a beautiful oak. We gave him drawings for a simple, minimalist design, but when he finally delivered we saw that he'd added his own flourish—a turned colonial-style trim, glued and nailed all over. He said it 'looked better' and refused to take it off. His attitude was bewildering but got me thinking about a lot of things relating to dogma, personal aesthetics and architectural space. The story took on its own life, but this incident was the trigger. (And the ugly trim is still there.)

## From the writers of Breaking Beauty ...

**Jessica Clements**
*'Olive/Oliver'*

A friend of mine was having a baby and it made me think about all the worry that comes with that as well as the potential complications. I wondered how someone would cope when things don't go the way they planned, both with the pregnancy and in their life at the time. This was partly how the structure came about also. I wanted to reflect the mother's emotional journey and the beauty of pregnancy in all its variations.

**Ruby Ewens**
*'Triangles, Squares and Circles'*

This story is like everything I write: I start with something simple and personal and then I become a bower-bird, stealing pretty things I find in my days. Books I'm reading, overheard conversations, smells and landscapes come into the frame. Whatever story is left may capture aspects of me, but the transformation breaks it away. This story is of a different time and place, playing with ideas that attempt to find both symmetry and conflict. I have had to resist the temptation to slice and dice it, to honour its original feeling, and let the editors work their magic to give it a second life.

**Heather Taylor Johnson**
***'Thank You, Jean Harley'***

My story is actually a self-contained chapter from my new novel manuscript *Jean Harley was Here.* In the book, Jean Harley is either in a coma or dead, so even though she is the novel's main character, she doesn't have a voice. It's up to the other characters in the book to bring Jean to life and prove that she indeed 'was here'.

**Mary Lynn Mather**
***'Whatever Happened to the Fairytale Ending?'***

As the title of the piece suggests, the starting point was one of those enduring stories from the Brothers Grimm. Some of the Sleeping Beauty images and motifs linger, but the end result is a tale of a different sort. It is lodged in the space where fantasy smacks against reality. That place where the mythical meets with the mundane is fascinating, especially when motherhood is thrown into the mix.

**Lilliana Rose**
***'Ladies Tea Party'***

I was watching an episode of Heston Blumenthal, and there was a rather different afternoon tea party where a small group of women were enjoying themselves with food: burlesque style. I wanted to mix this idea of a tea party with a bit more spice and a steampunk flavour to explore how women could choose to free themselves from social restrictions. I liked the idea of taking something so prim and proper as a social tea party and then turning it into something where the women weren't sitting down like ladies and drinking tea, gossiping, but instead were having the time of their lives expressing themselves without inhibitions.

**Anna Solding**
*'All You Need Is Love'*

My stories often start with an image. In this case I pictured a young man who had just been released from prison and had to make his own way home on a cold and windy winter's day. I imagined the story to be a chapter in my 'novel constellation' The Song of Glass, set in Malmö, Sweden, where I grew up. How does it feel to return to everyday life after being locked up? In 'All You Need Is Love' I wanted to explore addiction, loneliness and love and how the three are often intimately connected.

**Reg Taylor**
***'Something About Religion'***

Morbidity, the shocking intrusion of death that drowning provides, is part of my story. It's also inspired, I think, by the sympathy I have for strong female figures, whose tough outer skins sometimes conceal a sensitivity and vulnerability that experience has taught them to deny.

**Lynette Washington**
***'Lia and Amos'***

'Lia and Amos' came out of a conversation with friends about unconventional marriages, and how convention creates layers of expectation. Marriage is steeped in tradition. Some members of our society worry about it being preserved for heterosexual people, some worry about it fitting boundaries and rules, some dismiss it altogether. But it's a covenant between two consenting adults: shouldn't they be the ones to decide what the rules are? I like the idea of Lia and Amos doing something that might be considered dangerous, but doing it with love and support and respect and making it work for them.

**Bryan Whalen**
***'Duck'* and *'Self Portrait with Angel Olsen'***

'Duck' was written on a beach towel in the backyard of a friend's house on the Gold Coast. It came out in a single sitting and is the only story I've written than needed very few changes. Several years later, I moved to Adelaide to undertake a PhD in Creative Writing under the tutelage of Phillip Edmonds. I was living alone, in a cold apartment, my wife on the other side of the world, when I wrote 'Self Portrait with Angel Olsen'.

**Sean Williams**
***'The Beholders'***

'The Beholders' is an urban myth set in a universe where matter transmitters (think the teleporter from Star Trek) reign supreme. It seems inevitable to me that, given the capacity to take people apart and put them back together, the first use we put it to wouldn't be transportation, but body modification. Who doesn't want to be taller, faster, prettier, stronger? And nothing could possibly go wrong with *that*…

## MidnightSun Publishing

We are a small, independent publisher based in Adelaide, South Australia. Since publishing our first novel, Anna Solding's *The Hum of Concrete* in 2012, MidnightSun has gone from strength to strength.

We create books that are beautifully produced, unusual, sexy, funny and poignant. Books that challenge, excite, enrage and overwhelm. When readers tell us they have lost themselves in our stories, we rejoice in a job well done.

MidnightSun Publishing aims to reach new readers every year by consistently publishing excellent books. Welcome to the family!

**midnightsunpublishing.com**

***Publishing Brilliance***

www.ingramcontent.com/pod-product-compliance
Lightning Source LLC
Chambersburg PA
CBHW020759190726
48285CB00006B/2106

* 9 7 8 1 9 2 5 2 2 7 0 0 0 *